I0598324

Always and Forever Together

by

Dilys J Carnie

This is a work of fiction. Names, characters, places, and incidents are either the product of the author's imagination or are used fictitiously, and any resemblance to actual persons living or dead, business establishments, events, or locales, is entirely coincidental.

Always and Forever Together

COPYRIGHT © 2022 by Dilys J Carnie

All rights reserved. No part of this book may be used or reproduced in any manner whatsoever without written permission of the author or The Wild Rose Press, Inc. except in the case of brief quotations embodied in critical articles or reviews.
Contact Information: info@thewildrosepress.com

Cover Art by *Jennifer Greeff*

The Wild Rose Press, Inc.
PO Box 708
Adams Basin, NY 14410-0708
Visit us at www.thewildrosepress.com

Publishing History
First Edition, 2023
Trade Paperback ISBN 978-1-5092-4735-6
Digital ISBN 978-1-5092-4736-3

Published in the United States of America

It was the sexiest thing she'd ever seen as it hugged his slim hips. On closer inspection, his t-shirt had Steel Homes embroidered at the top right-hand corner below the collar. That seemed odd, Maisy thought; his last name was Steel. She took in the other details with the picture of a conifer tree with the words Pinewood Specialist, and she was about to ask him about it when she got sidetracked.

She seemed to have no control as her eyes roved down his body. She became very aware of his well-worn jeans and toe-scuffed boots.

"Oh," Maisy said because she didn't know what else to say.

"Uh-huh." His lips twitched in amusement. Jarrod tried so hard to keep from laughing at her expression of sheer embarrassment, but he lost the cause and gave out a full-belly laugh.

"I could easily change why I came over for that tête–à–tête you mentioned." She held up her hand, her cheeks red as she tried to speak, but no words came out. Then she put her hand to her forehead and groaned.

"I need coffee." And with those words, she turned around and headed to the kitchen. Elsa sat looking up at him. Jarrod went on his haunches and let the dog smell his hand before he stroked her soft fur. "Well, baby girl, she was a little touchy. Looks like she may be supporting a hangover, huh?"

Dedication

I dedicate this book to all those perpetually forever stories, love eternity, and happy endings.

And to my grandparents, who were married for sixty-eight years and still held hands. They were and still are my inspiration.

Acknowledgments

Thank you Wild Rose Press for finding a home for my books.

Chapter 1

Jarrod Steel stood on the veranda of his beach house, listening to the sound of the Atlantic Ocean. The waves were high today, but the wind was warm despite being September—unusually hot for this time of year in Nags Head. He lifted his cup of coffee and drank the now cooling liquid, his body tensed in anticipation. As the owner of Steel Homes, he made billion-dollar decisions with better discipline than he felt at this moment.

Where was she? Every morning for the last four days she'd walked past at a leisurely pace, her tousled pixie crop shining as the North Carolina sun brought out spun gold highlights. Her tanned legs had been on display with a pair of shorts fitted to show off a very nicely rounded ass. Her feet sank into the sand as she walked, her t-shirt flapping in the wind. A gorgeous golden retriever was at her side, never trotting too far away from her.

Jarrod frowned at the fantasies he'd had involving the mystery woman. Something about her stuck out in his mind, something vaguely familiar. He shook his head—surely, he would remember someone like her; her beauty would be unforgettable. Sucking in a deep breath, he blew the air back out slowly. He must be insane, watching and waiting for a woman he'd never met.

He usually didn't have a problem going after what he liked. But something about her went more profound, and he didn't know how to handle it deeper. She made him feel strange, protective, and even territorial. He had those instincts in business, but never over a woman, and especially one he didn't know.

Like an idiot, he waited every morning, watching like some psychotic stalker just to get a glimpse of her. It was too weird how he stood there staring and waiting, so instead, he turned and leaned against the railings. Folding his arms, he admired the house he had built with the help of his team of employees.

It covered four thousand seven hundred feet with storm and patio shutters that were remotely controlled during times of inclement weather. The two floors were spacious and kept to a beach house design. When sitting on the deck you could watch the sun set or rise beneath the shaded roof on the open porch. He'd loved doing all the woodwork, designing something and using his skills to treat himself.

At fifteen, he'd realized he was good with woodwork, and started making little wooden animals. He'd sold them in school, in the local market, anywhere that would buy them. The money he'd made accumulated quickly because he basically lived off nothing, spending as little money as possible. And as soon as he turned eighteen, he left the children's home and worked wherever he could find a job; construction, bar work and even cleaning.

It took him four years to save up enough to buy his first house, and with his connections working on several building sites, he had learned the craft of remodeling properties. It wasn't long before he had the ability to sell and buy. He'd spent the last twelve years building up his business.

Steel Homes was his passion; it was all about conserving what was around him. It had developed into a multi-billion-dollar business that specialized in turning old and forgotten homes into dream start-up houses for those who needed that first step on the ladder in life. Despite his status, he still liked to feel tools in his hands and sawdust against his skin as he worked. The satisfaction of carving something from nothing gave him great joy, which was why his homes were well known for their craftsmanship. He insisted his tradespeople use their craft and skills to produce their best work. To him it didn't matter if they were working on a hotel or a house for a first-time buyer, he expected the same quality from his employees.

He'd bought the plot of land in Nags Head intending to build something special, and he had. The view of the ocean was stunning, and being able to go down three steps and feel sand beneath his feet made him realize just how amazing his life had become. Growing up in DC, Jarrod had been passed from one foster home to another. He'd been lucky enough to spend a single vacation with his then-family by the beach.

He'd loved every minute of it, and promised himself that sometime in the future, he would return. He didn't need the private pool, or the seven bedrooms all en-suite, but he hadn't minded the million-dollar price tag. He could listen to the waves and watch the sunset while sitting on his veranda.

Setting the coffee cup on the outside patio table he'd made from driftwood picked up on the beach, he leaned his elbows on the wooden railings. He breathed the salty air deep into his lungs, his eyes hidden behind his sunglasses as the brightness of the morning sun beat down from the clear blue sky. Clasping his hands together, he gazed at the beautiful view. Jarrod never forgot how fortunate he was to have such a stunning property. The spectacular ocean views never ceased to take his breath away, and there weren't many things in his life that did that.

Jarrod worked diligently and expected his employees do the same, but he paid them well for their efforts. But now he'd reached a stage in his life where he wanted something more. He didn't quite believe—or perhaps he did, and hadn't wanted to acknowledge it—that the face of happily-ever-after might be out there for him.

Jarrod could stop working today and still have enough money to see him through the rest of his life comfortably. With some shrewd investments, his bank balance was something he need never think about. But what was the point in having all of this if there was no one to share it with? He could have his pick of numerous sophisticated, attractive women, but none of them had ever touched any of his emotions. He shook his head; his demeanor was crumbling. He cringed at thinking what Liam and Max, his longtime friends, would say if they knew what he was thinking. Yep, he'd keep those views to himself.

As Jarrod stood in the sunshine, he found his thoughts returning to the little blonde who had walked past his house. He'd only meant to stay a couple of days, but that had turned to four. He should be returning to his central office in Washington DC, and his apartment overlooking the Potomac River in Georgetown.

Straightening up to his full height, he saw her in the distance. His heart rate tripled, and he brushed his fingers through his hair. What was he doing pining after a woman he'd never met? Why was he spending every waking moment thinking about her? No woman had ever had him so tied up in knots before.

Jarrod had never felt this way. He embraced his single life with a passion, but just because he did, it didn't mean there was no such thing as a happy ever after and love. He'd never known his dad, and his mom had died of a drug overdose when he'd been twelve. Despite his latter teenage years in a children's home, he wasn't bitter about it. One day he wanted to get married and perhaps have children.

****

Maisy let her feet sink into the golden sand with every step she took; it was the most pleasurable experience. She loved the feeling of the warm sun on her face. It was like an explosion of happy sparkles floating through her body.

After relocating here, she had hoped to move on. She struggled every second of the day with a sadness that tore at her heart. Nighttime was the worst. She could always hear her own screams in her sleep, asking for her children, and it took every bit of strength she had to open her eyes each morning and face another day.

Relief had filled her when she'd bought her beach house. It carried happier teenage memories of when her parents had brought her here on holiday. They were good times. She'd been young, loved life, and looked forward to the future.

Little had she known how devastating it would be.

Maisy reached down to smooth the soft fur of the pet, who now shared the new home with her. Elsa, her loyal and steadfast friend, and Maisy was grateful for her company. Every time she said Elsa's name, she smiled at the memory of her daughter's insistence that they call the golden retriever Elsa from the movie *Frozen*. Not that Tom was impressed; he'd wanted to name the dog after a football player that Maisy couldn't pronounce.

After struggling to come to terms with what had happened the first summer, Maisy returned to work as a full-time art teacher, hoping it would kickstart her need to get into a routine. It hadn't taken long for her to realize everything she did was too much of a reminder. So, after persevering for over a year, she finally decided to sell the family home and make a new start.

When Maisy saw the beach house facing the Atlantic Ocean, she fell in love with it. Even after being warned of the hurricanes, she had no hesitation in telling the realtor, on the spot, that she'd buy it. And she did.

Her counselor had been pleased that she was finally looking forward and thought it good for her recovery to make plans. It was the right road for her to take; it was either that or ending up in a place where she could see no future for herself.

Her parents worried about her moving so far away, but she assured them she would be okay and Elsa would be with her. Maisy knew they were suffering their own feelings of loss. Without a doubt, her parents felt the devastation, so she encouraged them to take the world cruise they had planned.

When her first child, Tom, came along, someone had told her he would become the most precious thing in her life. And wasn't that the truth? And when Beth was born, she felt double blessed.

Losing them had been the worst thing ever.

But life had its way of pushing forward, making her

carry on come what may, even in those times when she wanted to give up. There had been many dark moments when she sought to end her life, to stop the pain, to stop the unforgiving emotions of not protecting the two things in her life that were most precious. The relentless help from her parents had kept her from doing anything that would hurt them more. They have already suffered the loss of their grandchildren.

As Maisy stood looking out into the ocean's vastness, she found it hard to believe her children were absent and not playing in the water, making sandcastles with buckets and spades. She shifted her gaze down to Elsa, who sat by her side. She was so close Maisy could feel her fur on her bare legs. Drawing her hand out of her shorts pocket, Maisy reached down to stroke Elsa's soft hair, the sun warm on her back.

Crouching down beside her, she whispered in her ear, "Go play in the water." But Elsa just looked at her with a pain in her eyes, one she was all too familiar with. Maisy knew that pain. She felt it every single day.

Elsa hadn't played at all since the accident. Maisy had gotten her because she thought it would be good for them to have a family pet. Elsa was a perfect dog and had been very protective of both Tom and Beth.

Standing up, Maisy continued with her daily walk, enjoying the quietness of the morning with only a few people scattering the beach. Taking a slight detour, she strolled toward the large, luxurious beach house, which was far bigger than her little beach dwelling.

As she got closer to the man watching her, she smiled at him. "Are you ever going to talk to me?" Maisy said to the man that had been pretending not to look at her.

****

Jarrod's heart almost stopped. Her soft British accent washed over him as it triggered memories of a summer vacation many years ago. Could it be? He lifted his sunglasses, settled them on top of his head, and looked at her face.

"Maisy?" he asked incredulously.

Lifting her sunglasses from her face, she giggled, and he recognized her straight away.

"Maisy Fields?" His mind went back fifteen years to one of the happiest times of his life, that vacation at the beach. She had laughed at his jokes as they'd had fun surfing the waves. She'd treated him like a buddy, whereas he had fantasized about her in an entirely different way for weeks, even months, after.

"The one and only," she replied with that inflection of humor in her voice—the same as it had been all those years ago.

"How long have you known it was me?" He couldn't contain the surprise in his voice.

"Oh, about the first time you hid behind your sunglasses, watching me."

Jarrod released an unsteady laugh. For the first time in his life, mortification made his skin prickle. "Damn, Maisy, why didn't you come over?"

"Because it was fun watching you pretend you weren't looking."

"Some things haven't changed then, always the tease," he said as the embarrassment gradually left him.

"You were always so easy to torment." She said it with a grin that made his heart flutter, just as it had all those years ago.

Oh boy, did he ever remember that fun-filled two

weeks when her parents had brought their only daughter to Nags Head on vacation. She'd been fifteen, and he'd been seventeen. Her long, blonde hair had cascaded down her back in soft curls. He had wanted her from the very first moment he'd seen her. He thought he would never recover when she returned to the UK. But he had.

"Do you want to come up?" he asked, hoping she'd say yes.

"Sure." She wrinkled her nose. "Do you mind if Elsa comes as well?" She reached down and scratched the golden retriever's ears, and although it was obvious the dog enjoyed the attention, she never took her eyes off Jarrod.

"Of course not." He offered his hand to help her step up onto the wooden decking. Maisy hesitated for a moment before setting her hand inside his large one. The dog growled softly, not taking his eyes off Jarrod. He wondered why the animal felt a need to protect her so much.

"It's okay, Elsa," she said, and although the dog took a long, measuring look at him, she remained silent and followed them up the steps. He felt bereft when Maisy removed her hand from his.

Jarrod drew out a chair for her, and she sat down. The golden-haired dog lay down by her feet, and he sat opposite Maisy. Wisps of her short hair blew with the warm wind. Her smooth complexion was makeup-free, and her nose and cheeks freckles stood out.

"I thought about you many times," Maisy said. "I wanted to write to you, but I didn't know what to say. We were thousands of miles apart, and what does one say in that situation? *I'm sorry I left without saying goodbye, and I didn't meet you that last night because it was too tough?"*

"It was fifteen years ago." He shrugged his shoulders, smiling. "At least you thought about me."

"How could I not think about you? We were friends. Those two weeks we spent together were precious. You taught me how to surf and beat those waves so I could swim in the Atlantic Ocean. Do you remember how often I fell trying to ride the waves?" She laughed.

He remembered the fun they'd had. He also recollected how often he'd come close to kissing her, but didn't have the courage.

"It was a magical time," she continued, "and only topped by the birth of my two children."

"You're married?" All of a sudden, his heart felt like a dead weight.

Even with the tan, she had, her skin went almost alabaster. She shook her head. "No, not anymore."

He waited for her to continue, but she turned her head toward the ocean. He tried not to stare at her, but he recalled how soft her long, blonde hair used to feel when the breeze blew it across his skin, melting him with a need she never knew.

One thing that hadn't changed were the summer freckles that had popped up on her nose and cheeks after spending long days in the sun. Cornflower blue eyes that once had sparkled now seemed sad, and her frame was thinner than he remembered. But she was definitely a woman now, instead of the girl who had sent his raging hormones into meltdown.

She leaned down to pet Elsa before turning back to face him. "So, you seem to have done well. This is a beautiful beach house."

"It's not mine. I'm staying here while I do some

work on it for the owner, who's a friend."

Why the hell did I just lie and say that?

"What kind of work do you do?" she asked.

"Carpentry. I made this table and the chairs."

"You did?" She let her hand trail along the top. "They're beautiful."

"I found the driftwood lying around the beach."

"You're a very talented man. I always knew you would do something with your hands." She reached across and laid hers over his extended one. "Strong but gentle."

A flood of memories ransacked his mind, memories that were always fun and forever unique. He turned his hand and wrapped his fingers around hers. The emotions he felt hit him square in the solar plexus so hard it took his breath away. Their eyes met, and for a moment, he held his breath before she smiled and let go.

He covered up his reactions to her touch by talking. "I was wild in those days, and didn't care what I did." He remembered how much he'd hated life, detested how he had lived, and loathed the system that had kept him there. Jarrod felt proud of what he'd achieved, yet knew he could have easily landed on the scrap heap.

His determination to be better than his parents had kept him going. Sleeping rough, working twenty-four-seven was all worth it now. The homes he built and sold were of good, sustainable value for young people starting out in life. He liked the thought that he gave them a rung on the ladder by producing the affordable properties he sold.

Maisy leaned back and looked at him. He felt her eyes taking in every line on his face.

"You haven't changed much," she said. "I knew it

was you as soon as I saw you. Your hair is a lot shorter, but otherwise, you look the same."

"You make me feel like a louse for not recognizing you."

"Nah, don't. I have changed, so I'll forgive you." She had a twinkle in her eyes. "But only if you never tell me how many more age lines I have." Her laughter sang through the wind, making his heart flutter.

"You're still beautiful."

She blushed a little and smiled. "Thank you. So, tell me, are you married, kids?"

He shook his head. "Never seemed to have the time."

They sat for a moment, the silence uncomfortable, and he searched his mind for something to say. Who would believe he was the same man who gave orders and sat in million-dollar business meetings when he was as tongue-tied as the first day he had met her.

"Well, I'd better go." She stood up, followed by her dog, and Jarrod did the same.

He looked at her as she slipped her glasses from her head, but not before their eyes connected with a keen sense of awareness that left his heartbeat pounding. He followed her down onto the beach, trying desperately to keep his gaze straight ahead. *Damn.* He drew his sunglasses from the top of his head and slipped them on. But only after he'd quickly glanced down at her small, perfectly rounded butt. He could almost feel his retinas burn with his lack of control.

As she turned around to say goodbye, he shoved his hands into his shorts pockets and forced them to stay there.

"It was good to see you again, Jarrod, really good."

She smiled and walked away, Elsa at her side, trotting contentedly.

"Hey, where are you staying?" he shouted against the warm breeze.

"I have a place about a mile down the beach."

"Can I call on you?"

"Please do. You won't miss the house, just look for the almost derelict one." She laughed before turning and walking away.

****

Each morning was the same for Maisy, waking up with an aching heart for a few seconds. She stretched her legs from the curled-up position she had woken in and took a moment to get her bearings.

Sometimes she didn't want to sleep, so she didn't have to go through those moments in the morning when she realized it hadn't been a horrific nightmare. A picture of her sweet little babies sat on her bedside table—an image of the three of them all huddled together because it had been cold on the beach. A fun, happy day despite the weather.

The tears still came, but they were less like the heartbreaking sobs that used to rack her body. Her salvation had originated from her counselor Lynn, and when she'd decided to make this move, Lynn had said that, finally, she was moving on.

Maisy guessed it was true that time did help, but maybe she didn't want it to work totally. Perhaps feeling this way took away the responsibility she felt at being unable to save Tom and Beth, and she didn't want to lose that guilt. But most of all, she still couldn't take away the sense of blame she felt for not dying with them.

Maisy should have known. She should have stopped

Jack.

He'd picked up Tom, Beth, and Maisy from school, to take them back to the house so the children could pick up their weekend cases. It had been her ex-husband's turn to have them, although that didn't always work out that way, as he often forgot. Too late she realized he'd been drinking when he'd gotten behind the wheel of the car.

Jack misjudged a corner, rolling the car over and over again... She often relived the screams, the sound of metal crunching, and the absolute terror of trying to reach for her children. It seemed to go on forever, but it all happened in twenty seconds, according to the driver of the car behind them. Now she still had to endure the court case, which was coming up in four weeks.

Maisy was grateful for each and every day she had the company of her canine companion. Before, she'd never allowed her to sleep on her bed. Her husband Jack would never let her, although she knew sometimes Elsa sneaked into Beth's room and crawled into her bed. Now Elsa slept tucked against Maisy every night, giving each other comfort when needed.

She'd come to this part of North Carolina determined to make a life for herself. Once she'd gotten past that first, awful Christmas without her children, Maisy tried to go back to working as a teacher in the village she lived in. But it had been unbearable seeing Tom and Beth's friends every time she came to work. Mothers she'd once spent coffee mornings with now didn't know what to say to her.

It hadn't taken long for her to realize it wasn't going to work. She'd loved her job, but it hindered her recovery, because there were too many memories.

Enduring the pitying gazes, and the silences when no one knew what to say to her was an agony she couldn't take. So she'd emptied her locker, cleared her desk, and said goodbye.

Her parents were worried sick about her move, but she promised to email them and ring when she could, and the affirmation seemed to pacify them. Sending them on their way had been hard, but the cruise they'd been planning long before this happened would do them a world of good.

Just over fourteen months had passed since that awful day. Maisy closed her eyes as she felt every second of that time. Life had a frustrating way of moving forward, with or without you, forcing you to flow with it when it would have been so much easier not to.

Turning over, she swung her legs to the floor and stared at the ground, a tear finding its way onto her bare leg. Sometimes it was hard for her to believe they were gone. She shifted her gaze to the window and the vast span of the ocean beyond, which seemed close enough to touch.

Every time she looked, it was like seeing a brand new view. Soon there would be surfers and beach people covering the sands. The surf rode high. She remembered how it used to toss her around. Jarrod would laugh and lift her as if she weighed nothing, until they'd got past the vigorous waters into the calmer part of the ocean where they would swim and play. It all seemed like a lifetime ago…it was.

Seeing him yesterday had brought back so many happy memories. It didn't surprise Maisy that he was still as gorgeous as he had been all those years ago, even more so if at all possible. Soft green eyes, dark blond hair streaked by the sun as it fell against his tanned forehead, and those lips…holy cow, they were made for kissing.

Maisy stood up and stretched before padding her way through the small house with only a bedroom, bathroom, living room, and kitchen. She laughed at the thought. *Kitchen* was an overstatement. The realtor had warned her of the property's sparsity. Only one cupboard which was almost detached from the wall, a sink, and a refrigerator. The stove she had bought when moving in.

Maisy switched on the kettle for her tea, walked back through the house, and opened the locked door which led to her porch. She breathed in the sharp scent of the ocean, feeling the breeze on her skin as she listened to the sound of waves swishing against each other.

The clear blue sky, marked only by the golden sun beating down onto the sand, made it very clear why she'd paid for a beach house that had seen better years. The early morning only saw a few people—some joggers and walkers. Her reclusive lifestyle had been a decision she made; it was the only way to get herself together.

Over to her right stood Jeannette's Pier, with the surf breaking hard against the concrete pilings that kept it above water. The new construction was pretty impressive; she'd seen pictures of Hurricane Isabel's damage.

The pier house stood tall and strong enough to withstand anything. A few fishermen sat on the end, hoping to catch some skates or dogfish: older men, happy to sit and listen to the waves crash beneath them.

Close to the shore were the ever-present dolphins, swimming and playing, putting on a show for whoever would stop and take the time to watch them. She didn't deserve all this when her children weren't there to share it with her.

She felt the ever-presence of Elsa at her side and reached down and stroked her. Elsa looked up at Maisy.

"What shall we do today, buddy?"

The dog barked, then went out onto her tiny front yard and did her business before coming straight back to her side. Elsa sighed as she stretched out on the decking, and Maisy laughed.

"That figures, same as normal then, a lazy day in the sun." Taking a deep breath, Maisy turned and went back inside. Perhaps she would paint today.

Chapter 2

Jarrod questioned his decision to go running at this time of the day. The beach was busy as the sun beat down against his back. It was the millionth time he'd thought of Maisy since yesterday. For the first time in his life, he felt uncertain.

He didn't know which house belonged to her, but he guessed it would be somewhat recognizable by her description. As he looked toward the many beach houses, they all seemed to be in good, sound order.

Maisy had always treated him like a buddy, but he had other fantasies in mind, like kissing her. He'd been a horny seventeen-year-old, but now, at twice that age, his hormones still raged through his body.

He wondered if her children were with her. Some of these houses were vacation rentals, but there were a few bought ones, and if she'd purchased the property, maybe she had ideas about moving here permanently. Damn, he was constantly thinking about her. He should have headed back to DC, where he knew a mountain of work awaited him.

His t-shirt flapped in the wind, the breeze warm from the ocean, and he realized it had been a while since he'd run, usually preferring to use the gym in the basement. He wasn't acting his usual, practical self, and he cursed the reasons behind this defect in his character. Every time he thought about their conversation it made his heart flutter. Maisy remembered him. He laughed softly as he crossed the sands at a slow pace, making his way toward some houses slightly set back from the beach.

She did ask him to call on her, so how rude would it be not to? But was it too soon to respond to the invitation? He had wanted to go after her yesterday but refrained from looking like a complete sap.

Jarrod spent the rest of yesterday working on some carvings for a workshop. He was involved with a children's home where he donated his time and money, helping kids realize their potential. He never forgot how lucky he'd been to be able to make a success of his life, and he wanted to give back some of what he had to those who were struggling. Jarrod remembered all too well how lonely and pathetic he had felt when he'd been left alone.

The work was with a group of fifteen-year-old boys who were being allowed to learn a skill. Boys who were more practical than theoretical, and he was showing them by example how sheer determination and hard work brought you anything you wanted.

When Jarrod called his secretary that morning, she'd asked if he was all right. He hadn't been surprised by the question. Sheena had been with him for nearly ten years and wasn't afraid to speak her mind. As she correctly pointed out, he'd been due four days ago, and staying away from the business he loved to run was unlike him. She'd picked up on the disquiet coming across on the phone; he could sense her surprise at his unplanned time off.

"You're distracted, Jarrod. I can hear it in your voice. What's wrong?" Sheena had spoken, some would

say, out of turn. But he knew her concern had been for him. Jarrod told her he was fine and had decided to take some time off. He chuckled because he knew she would never believe that.

But Sheena was correct, he was distracted. He could still smell Maisy, feel the touch of her hand on his, and how small it felt next to his. It showed a delicacy about her that he liked, but he felt she was a lot stronger than she looked.

Jarrod could be setting himself up for one hell of a disappointment. What would happen when he went back home? Would she return to the UK, or was she here to stay? And if staying, did he have a chance with her? Wasn't he just torturing himself with what he wanted but couldn't have?

Hell yeah! But that didn't stop him. Jarrod couldn't shake off the thought of spending time with someone who made his heart beat so fast he felt like he'd done an hour in the gym.

As he looked to the right, he saw a property smaller than the rest, almost on the beach, with a tiny yard at the front, surrounded by beach-washed fencing that needed painting. Wooden lattice surrounded the back entrance with steps leading up to the porch. The wooden building looked like it had been through a few rough storms. Either side of the door was a window, nothing fancy, with white wooden frames that needed to be replaced.

Jarrod stopped in front of the gate, hands on hips, trying to catch his breath. He took a swig from the bottled water he'd been carrying. God damn, it was hot!

He opened the small latch gate separating her yard from the beach and headed up the path to her porch. The house needed some work—a lot of work Someone had filled boxes with colorful plants were set against the front of the property, and the array of the sweet-smelling flowers titillated his senses.

He suddenly stopped at the steps to the porch because she was sitting cross-legged, her hands upturned on her knees with her eyes closed. Maisy had been hidden behind the lattice woodwork that surrounded her porch. Maisy was meditating with Elsa at her side. The dog lazily watched Jarrod quietly take the four steps onto the deck.

In a pair of denim shorts and a yellow t-shirt, Maisy looked serene and relaxed. He couldn't take his eyes off her. Her breathing was slow and quiet, and the sound of the ocean in the background gave the whole aura a carpet of tranquility. Just looking at her made him feel stress-free.

"You know you could give me an inferiority complex by watching me."

Her voice startled him, and he felt almost stalkerish. Her eyes opened, and stared back at him with a playful twinkle. The expression on her face took him back to teenage memories, which, after years of not thinking about her, besieged him all at once. He remembered how she had the ability always to make him smile. In his teenage years he'd rarely laughed but she'd made him feel happy, and playful, like he'd never done any of those things before. Well, he hadn't. Maisy gave him faith in human nature; she hadn't cared where he'd come from, or what he had.

She'd plied him with friendship and made him laugh until he thought he'd never stop. Most of all she made him happy, and at that time, happiness had been severely lacking in his life. He'd been more talkative with her than with any counselor the authorities had tried to push him into seeing.

"Jarrod?"

He snapped out of his somewhat confusing state to find her smiling back at him.

"Now that you're here, would you like something to drink, or are you just going to stand there?" She stood up, and her smile turned into concern.

"That would be nice, thanks. Do you mind?"

"Of course not, I was hoping you would, although this…" She spread her arms. "This is nothing like what you are used to."

"How do you know what I'm used to?" he asked.

She shrugged. "You're right. I shouldn't have assumed. I'm sorry."

Now Jarrod felt bad, because not only had he lied to her about the house, but he'd insinuated she was wrong, and she wasn't. His money could buy him a lifestyle so different from Maisy's, and he should have told her then and there. But he didn't…coward.

"Let's go inside, and I'll make us a drink." She gestured for him to follow her.

Jarrod reached down and petted the animal beside her. "She follows you everywhere."

"Yes, she's very protective."

The screen door banged behind him. He was almost too big for the room he assumed was the living room. With only a small two-seater sofa and a large rug on the wooden flooring, it was sparse, to say the least. Some boxes and a covered easel by the window were piled in a corner.

She continued into the next room. There was no door where there should have been one. The kitchen needed complete overhauling. Jarrod shoved his hands into his shorts pockets. As she turned, there wasn't time to lose the pity in his eyes.

"This is my choice," she said. "I could have stayed in the UK, bought more for my money, or moved to a different part of the States and had a comfortable condo. But I didn't want all that—all I need is this. The house needs renovations, but I haven't gotten around to it yet."

He frowned, not sure what to make of what she'd said. Didn't she say yesterday that she had children?

"My kids, Tom and Beth, died in a car crash fourteen months ago," she said in answer to his silent query.

He couldn't stop the shock from showing in his face. Jarrod's heart ached at the pain in her voice and the shock he felt at something so utterly horrific. "Jesus, Maisy, I'm so sorry."

"I know, and it's okay. I'm slowly coming to terms with what happened. Well, that's what I try to tell myself." She squeezed her eyes shut, just a small motion, but the pain was so apparent in the contour of her face, it stabbed at his heart. "Until I wake up in the morning, when, for a split second, I expect them both to jump onto my bed for morning cuddles. And then...and then the realization hits me, and I know that will never happen again. I'm not sure if I will ever get over it."

Jarrod was shocked; it was probably one of the worst things he'd ever heard. Saying 'sorry' just couldn't convey how sad he felt for her, and he didn't know how to express that, so he said nothing.

"Cold sweet tea?" she asked as she opened the refrigerator.

"Yes, please." He watched as she removed a jug

from the refrigerator, took two glasses from the cupboard, then filled them and handed him a glass.

Taking hers, she beckoned him to follow her. "Come on, let's sit outside on the porch."

He followed her and sat in one of the two chairs facing the ocean. Elsa flopped down on the floor next to her feet. Maisy reached down and scratched behind her ears.

"She has never recovered from them not coming home. I had her before my babies were born. She loved to play with them and cuddle up to them, and now she's as lost as I am without them. Which is why she follows me everywhere." She sipped her drink before setting it down onto the small table between them. "Poor thing. Elsa has been through a lot."

It seemed to Jarrod that Maisy had been to hell and back. He chose not to say anything because she certainly wouldn't have needed reminding.

****

Maisy looked out at the waves as they crashed against the sand, the white froth dispersing time after time. The beach began to fill with people, and surfers were on the water, vying for the largest wave to take them on a mind-boggling ride.

She gave Jarrod a sideways glance, allowing him time to digest what she'd told him. It was never easy telling her story. She'd done it a hundred times—police, courts, solicitors, friends, co-workers…the list became endless. Time was supposed to be a great healer, but she didn't think that any amount of time would ever heal and close the gaping hole left by the loss of her children.

"It's a beautiful day," she said.

"Maisy?"

"Yes?"

"Tell me what happened…if it's not too painful."

Why had she blurted it out like that? This man had the ability to make her feel so at ease. "My husband and I are divorced, and it was his weekend to have the children. I taught at the same school my children went to so when he picked them up after school I rode with them so they could go get their packs."

"You don't drive?"

"Yes, but my car was in the garage having a service. We lived close to the school so we had walked there that morning. Jack had a Range Rover with all the gadgets, and Tom loved to sit in the front, so he was in the passenger seat on his booster cushion. I got into the back with Beth." She'd gone over this scenario time and time again.

"Don't do that. You can't blame yourself."

"I can, and I do. Jack, my ex-husband, had flair, and flamboyancy. He'd been born with a silver spoon in his mouth. He never had to work because Mummy and Daddy provided well for their only son."

"But you worked?"

She nodded. "Yes, I'm an art teacher. Although Jack provided a substantial child allowance—and he reminded me frequently that he paid it—I never used that to live on. It was invested into an account for Tom and Beth, for their future." She trailed off and, for a second, said nothing. "He wasn't averse to having long, liquid lunches, but I never thought for one moment he would drink when he knew he had the children."

She gripped the arms of the wooden beach chair, and although the temperature had reached the seventies and above, she felt pretty cold as the scenario played over in her head.

"You know, it's the little things I remember. My counselor says it's because I'm trying to block out what happened, but that isn't true."

Her lips felt dry. She removed the lip balm from her shorts pocket, smoothing it across the dryness.

"The sound of Beth chattering about the school, and how they had made biscuits with faces on them. Her giggle sounded like chimes blowing in the wind. The car window had been open a little, and every time she turned to look out, it blew her blonde fringe back from her chubby, little face. I remember her beautiful mouth as her lips moved in speech, never seeming to take a breath. She could talk the hind legs off a donkey." She laughed. "Even in sleep, she would talk. Tom was more the silent type, always had his head stuck in a book. Which he was doing when it happened."

"You don't have to say anymore, Maisy."

"I do, I want you to know." She wasn't entirely sure why she felt the need to tell all the details to Jarrod, a man she hadn't seen in fifteen years, but she had always felt comfortable with him. Despite his childhood, he had a side to him that was caring and understanding, and based on the concerned look in his sea-green eyes, she didn't think he had changed much.

"I hope they didn't feel a thing when Jack overturned the car because he took a corner too wide." Big tears sat in her eyes as she willed them to stay where they were. "I remember screams and reaching to put my arms around Beth." She rubbed her forehead. "It felt as though it went on for hours. But later, the police told me, based on witness statements, that it had only been a matter of seconds before the car stopped." She bowed her head before looking at Jarrod. "Beth and Tom were dead on impact. Jack and I survived. It should have been *us* lying in the morgue. A child should *never* die before their parents. It's just not right."

"You were uninjured?"

"Jack had some whiplash, cuts, and bruises, and I had a broken pelvis and two broken ribs from where the seatbelt tightened."

"So, Jack was found to have been drinking?"

"Yes, they do an alcohol and drug test whenever an accident occurs. Jack was twice over the legal limit."

"The police arrested him?"

"Yes, and his parents bailed him out. I have to go back to the UK the end of September for the final court hearing. I hope they sentence him."

"Why has it taken so long?"

"Because they can afford the best." Maisy stood, stepped over to the porch railing and leaned against it. She gave a bitter laugh. "They never liked me. I wasn't good enough for their perfect son. But they loved their grandchildren." A tremor ran through her body.

"I don't know if I'll ever forgive him. But I understand why his parents are helping him the way they are doing."

"You always were kindhearted."

"No, no. I'm just a woman trying to survive without too much bitterness inside me." Some days she managed to achieve that. For others, it was like trekking in quicksand. Elsa watched her every move as if she had a sixth sense that told her she had to take care of Maisy now.

Seeming to realize she was going to sink into the doom and gloom which had followed her for the last fourteen months, Jarrod stood and took her arm. "Come and show me your home. Perhaps I can help you with some of the work."

She looked surprised at him. "You would do that? Do you have time?"

"I always have time for old friends."

"Thank you, Jarrod. That's so sweet of you."

Her stomach quivered when he smiled at her. For a moment, she held his gaze, and her body reacted in a way she hadn't felt in a long time. Maisy was aware of his calloused hand at her back as he ushered her toward the door.

Warmth engulfed her, and her breath caught in her throat as she looked back up at him. She saw something different in those eyes, and she wasn't sure who leaned into whom, but she knew that if the world had ended, she couldn't have moved from that spot.

His hand settled on her shoulder as his thumb swept over her nape, tipping her head so her gaze was connected directly with those gorgeous eyes. Instinctively, she put both her hands on his chest. He kissed her, a soft, brushing kiss that wasn't enough for her. The sound she heard was her moan, and she pulled back, shocked at what had happened.

Jarrod studied her raptly, his thumb caressing her skin. "Uh-huh, that's better."

She frowned. "What do you mean?"

"Your eyes were sad," he said. "You can't keep blaming yourself for something that isn't your fault. I can't pretend to know what you went through, but at some point, you have to start living again."

Maisy pulled away. Elsa seemed to sense something was wrong and growled as Jarrod stood at her side.

"Down, girl." She let her hand drop to the dog's head and smooth the fur.

Jarrod gently pulled her back toward him. "Is that dog going to bite me if I try that again?"

He didn't give her a chance to reply because his lips were already on hers, and her eyes automatically drifted shut. Boy, he knew how to kiss. She'd often wondered all those years ago what those lips would be like, and now she knew. The kiss persisted, hot and profound, his taste, his touch, the heat emanating from his body—it was everything she hadn't felt for a long time.

Was it such a bad thing that she wanted to live a little and enjoy the moment? Didn't she deserve a moment like this? But permitting herself...that was the hard thing. However, she couldn't help but smooth her hands up and around his neck, her fingers threading into his hair.

The growl of approval reverberating from his throat mixed with hers, and she thought right then that this had been the most enjoyment she'd had in such a long time.

"Damn, I haven't made out at the beach in forever," he said as she slowly pulled apart from him. His voice was low and gruff. "Give yourself the chance to be happy."

"I've never made out on the beach," she said with a shaky laugh, feeling a lightness in her body, the empowerment giving her a sense of freedom, perhaps because it had been so long since she had allowed herself to think like that.

As she tried to move away, his hand on her waist tightened slightly. "Makes me real glad I'm your first," Jarrod said with a mischievous glint in his eye.

He moved his other hand so both gripped her hips as

if to move her closer, but she pulled back. Maisy felt a little uncomfortable. Every time she tried to be happy, she could only think of what she had lost.

"You don't want this," she said to him, hoping he didn't, yet some of her hoped he did.

"I beg to differ."

Her gaze traveled down his body, past his broad chest, over the flat abs she had felt beneath her fingertips, to the bulge clearly straining behind his shorts. She felt him watching her and immediately looked back at his face. Her embarrassment must have shown because his lips lifted in an amused smile.

Goodness! She could feel her cheeks burning! How old was she? Maisy had never felt such an instant sexual attraction to a man before, and it shocked her a little. After what she had been through, she seriously thought she never wanted to feel happy again.

"Oh God," she whispered.

Her children were barely cold in their graves, and her mind was filled with enjoyment; she was thinking about her pleasure. No, no. She didn't want to feel any of those things. She drew away from him, and he let her. It was enough room to give her breathing space, and she felt the wood of the porch railing at her back as she pressed hard into it. The soft breeze blew around her legs, relishing it on her hot skin.

"I think...you should go," she said without looking at him. Maisy could feel his eyes on her. She didn't want to see what he was thinking.

"Sure, I'll go, but I'll be back to look at what refurbishments you need."

"There's no need."

He stopped beside her at the top of the steps. "I said

I would."

"But I…"

"What? Don't you think you should have a little happiness in your life?"

"It's not the way I want to lead my life. I just want to be left alone."

"Maisy…" He bent down and gently brushed a kiss over her lips, moving slowly back and forth.

"Oh God," she whispered. "You're not playing fair."

"All's fair in love and war," he said, leaving her standing there as he made his way out of her yard.

****

Jarrod had never been able to stay in bed late. He rose with the sun every morning. If he'd been at home, he would have hit the gym, but it was a shame not to enjoy the beautiful location. The early morning had a coolness in the air, but judging by the blue sky, it was going to get much warmer.

He stood for a moment, looking out at the ocean. The surf was impressive, and the memory of riding the wave as it came in strong and powerful reminded him that it had been a while since he had done it. To be at one with the most controlling commodity on this planet was exciting. The exhilaration and freedom were like nothing else he'd ever experienced, except perhaps when he carved something from nothing.

His simple lifestyle helped keep him grounded, despite having enough money never to work again. This beach house had been his first extravagant buy ever, totally different to the properties he bought and sold. It was his luxury, and he hadn't regretted one single overpaid dollar it cost him.

It had taken him a long time to forgive himself for not being the type of son who made parents stick around just for a child's love. He'd long ago decided a love like that didn't exist for him, and he would never allow himself to be hurt the way he'd been as a young boy growing up.

Until he'd met Maisy again. That was a whole different story; the emotions he felt were frighteningly real, and the shock went deep into his soul. The slight, blonde woman with the endearing quality of an unconscious warmth, and inherent sexiness, despite her eyes of sadness, haunted the hell out of him.

A disturbing blend.

He pulled on his sports gear, slipped out onto the deck, and did a few stretches before running along the beach from one end to the other. He took a dip in the ocean which wasn't yet warm, but he enjoyed the coldness against his overheated skin. There weren't many people out and about at this time. The swooping seagulls still patrolled the length and breadth looking for any scraps left overnight.

Jarrod was hardly out of breath when he ran past the gazebo and up the path leading to his back entrance. He went through the door into the house.

After Maisy told him about what happened to her children, he had no idea how she must feel. It made him understand how he'd never felt pain as traumatic as hers. He liked a lot of people, and a lot of things, but love? He had everything he could ever want, and could buy anything he wanted, but his discombobulated mind never allowed him to get too involved, or care too much. He realized now that it was a sentence he'd served on himself since he'd been left alone.

How could Maisy be feeling to have lost the two things that had been a part of her body? It must have been like tearing out her heart. Did it make her who she was? To go through such pain should have been life-destroying, but she was getting through it; she seemed to be surviving the sadness. He felt a surge of admiration for her.

But it wasn't just respect he felt for her, it was what he'd felt all those years ago—a connection. But it felt like much more than that, and it scared the pants off him. He took a steadying breath and smoothed his fingers through his damp hair.

When he'd kissed Maisy, it seemed like the most natural thing in the world to do. He didn't usually shy away from women. For some reason, they liked him, and he greatly enjoyed the female company. But that one kiss with her had wrought the most potent emotion he'd ever felt.

Somewhere along his life, he'd forgotten what it was like to love or be loved. Jarrod didn't remember his dad. He couldn't remember a time when his mom hadn't taken some form of drugs, and as he got older he realized that her dependency ruled her life, ruled his life growing up.

Jarrod had hated her for so long he couldn't remember when he'd forgiven her, and for a moment, he was shocked to discover that was what he'd done. How had the knowledge passed him by and the wherewithal to be at peace, not only with himself but with the life he'd managed to leave behind years ago?

When Jarrod had listened to Maisy's story his heart melted at the very sight of her still struggling to come to terms with her losses. When he'd kissed her it had been an impulsive moment—one he did not regret for one moment.

Jarrod promised he'd help with the renovations, but he wasn't sure if she would welcome him after yesterday. Striding through the house, he went straight to the master bathroom adjoining his room and turned on the shower. Shedding his clothes, he stepped in and let the cold water gush onto his body.

He had a plan…

Chapter 3

For a moment Maisy lay there, the loud banging scaring the crap out of her. Totally disoriented, she sat up and looked around her, a haze covering her eyes. Were Beth and Tom right in front of her? She blinked, and then blinked again, before she comprehended they weren't there. Only her imagination playing tricks with her sorrow, wishful thinking that they were with her.

Closing her eyes to her pounding headache, Maisy waited for the wave of deep sadness to engulf her, and it didn't let her down. She was trembling as she swung her legs out of bed. Elsa extricated herself from the other half of the bed with a stretch and a yawn.

Maisy rubbed the back of her stiff neck. It wasn't unusual for her to wake up in the morning with a few aches and pains. Evidently, the pounding drum in her head was the work of a whole bottle of wine she had consumed last night while painting.

The creeping years made her less able to cope with the horrible hangover she seemed to have. With a groan, she stood up, and nearly toppled back onto the bed. Slapping a hand on the nearby wall, she opened one eye, then another, looked down at herself, and groaned. Her shorts had marks of the golden yellow and green oil paint she'd been using last night. So much so that Maisy couldn't even say what color they were.

She brushed her fingers through her short hair. They

became stuck on what she could only assume was dried-in paint. She walked from her bedroom to the living room and over to her easel. On the floor staring back at her was the photograph of her babies.

It constantly weighed on her mind that she'd forget what they looked like, so she'd decided to paint a portrait of them together; it would be her reminder of how she remembered them. Maisy had delved in her box of pictures, because she didn't want to forget a curve, a freckle, or any tiny part of them. But she didn't need a picture, at least not now. She could still paint them from her memories. Precious recollections had made her paint until the early hours of the morning. Maisy looked at the canvas and smiled at the two faces grinning back at her. Yes, she had captured them perfectly.

There was a knock at the door, and she quickly covered the painting up. In unison, she and Elsa both made a beeline for the door. She almost fell flat on her face as the dog moved in front of her.

Catching sight of herself in the seashell mirror over the small table by the door, she placed her hand over her mouth to stop herself from squealing out loud. Her hair was a mixture of green and yellow paint. She even had it down one side of her face, which looked much worse due to a crease down her cheek that must have come from the way she slept. *Damn!* She looked like she'd fought with a paint pot.

"Never again. Not one more drop of alcohol shall pass these lips. Water only from now on," she whispered while scowling at her reflection.

Elsa sat at her feet and watched her as if she'd gone mad. Maisy concluded she had.

"I know," Maisy said, looking at her. "I shouldn't

have drank the whole bottle."

She leaned over to look out the open window, and Jarrod grinned at her. He winked playfully as he said, "Hi."

Elsa jumped up when she saw someone at the window, knocking Maisy over, and she tumbled to the floor.

"Oh my God," she shrieked as she landed on hard on her ass, Elsa licking her face.

"Hey, are you okay?" Jarrod asked as he opened the door. She couldn't believe she'd left the door unlocked, but then again she had been tipsy, so it shouldn't have surprised her.

The giant of a man leaned over her. Wearing well-worn Levis, a white t-shirt, sunglasses, and a sheepish smile, he was all male.

Maisy stared up at him, feeling small, and like a fool for just lying there, but she couldn't help it. He was so damn tall, and oozed sex, damn him. She was still drunk, she must be. She wanted it to be a dream, and not actual. Geez, this day was starting great.

"Elsa, get off, you great big lummox." She pushed her dog to one side.

Elsa sat looking at her with ears perked up.

"It's okay, baby. I'm all right." She caressed Elsa's head as she sat up. "Yes, I'm great, thanks," she answered Jarrod in a sarcastic tone as his large hands held her arms and helped her to her feet.

Taking off his sunglasses, Jarrod leaned down to look into her face with concern. With his gaze focused on her, Maisy tried not to stare back into those green orbs that had always been her downfall. She knew how wild she must have appeared, but to give him credit, he didn't say a word.

His eyes were tinged with heat as they gazed at her parted lips, and no doubt he recalled the hot kiss they had shared. Hell, she remembered it just as well. Suddenly it was all she could think about: deep, delicious kisses.

His hands on her skin reminded her of how he'd touched her, and the tingling in her lower abdomen was heading in a direction she hadn't felt in a very long time.

"Hey, you sure you're okay?" he asked.

Oh, absolutely, on top of the world this morning. One thing she had to do was make it clear about last night. Because as much as she'd enjoyed meeting up with him, and, er, other things—even that goofy smile he had on his face now—she had to be honest with him.

She stepped back so she could be released from his hold. "About last night," she said as she clasped her hands together in front of her. "If I gave you the impression I was ready for..." Swallowing, Maisy couldn't look at him. She was so embarrassed she could feel her cheeks heating up.

"Kiss," he said, and she could hear the teasing tone in his voice.

"Yes, the kiss, I'm not in the right frame of mind for anything like that."

Jarrod didn't speak, and it unnerved her; the silence was awful and made her feel much worse than the pounding headache she had from the hangover.

"It's nothing personal. You understand from what I told you yesterday, I'm not in that sort of place."

He didn't say anything, just to look at her, making her feel mightily uncomfortable because Maisy knew she had lied to herself. Because who wouldn't be interested in Mr. Handsome? Quite clearly, only someone who had on a blindfold.

She slid him a guarded look. "Look, Jarrod, I know I may have led you on, and I'm sorry, but seriously, I have nothing to offer you."

Maisy could tell he was fighting a smile. He reached down and slipped his fingers through her short hair. Mortification crept all the way to the tips of her toes when he pulled a lump of paint from the strands that were sticking up.

"I was painting until late last night," she explained.

He lifted an eyebrow and looked around the room.

"No, not the walls. I paint…you know, portraits, landscapes, anything."

Maisy realized she sounded like an out-of-breath schoolgirl; time to pull herself together. And, hey, she didn't have to explain how she looked or what she did to anyone.

"Can I see?"

She shook her head. "No."

When Elsa whined, she realized the poor dog was almost crossing her legs, so she opened the door for her to go out to the small yard. Turning back to the man who was far too tall and big for her little house, she folded her arms across her chest. Maisy noticed his eyes following her actions. She realized why as her nipples felt more than a little firm against the material of her t-shirt. Maisy *knew* he'd seen them.

"You've had a wasted journey."

"I have?" He raised an eyebrow.

Maisy nodded. "Yes, you see, there's never going to be a repeat of last night."

She expected she might get struck by lightning for saying something that wasn't entirely accurate. Jarrod stared back at her. Spellbound, she nearly jumped ten feet when Elsa barged back through the door and sat at her side. When she saw Maisy wasn't moving, she flopped on her belly beside her bare feet. A deafening silence bounced around the room as Maisy waited for Jarrod to say something.

Finally, he spoke. "I'm happy to abide by your rules. However, I'm not here to repeat last night's little *tête–à– tête*."

"You're not?" A feeling of embarrassment overwhelmed her as she remembered how she'd just rattled on.

"No, I'm here to do what I said I would."

She frowned. Jarrod took a hammer from the belt she now noticed. Yep, a tool belt It was the sexiest thing she'd ever seen as it hugged his slim hips.

On closer inspection, his t-shirt had *Steel Homes* embroidered at the top right-hand corner below the collar. That seemed odd, Maisy thought; his last name was Steel. She took in the other details with the picture of a conifer tree with the words *Pinewood Specialist*, and she was about to ask him about it when she got sidetracked. She seemed to have no control as her eyes roved down his body. She became very aware of his well-worn jeans and toe-scuffed boots.

"Oh," Maisy said because she didn't know what else to say.

"Uh-huh." His lips twitched in amusement.

****

Jarrod tried so hard to keep from laughing at her expression of sheer embarrassment, but he lost the cause and gave out a full-belly laugh.

"I could easily change why I came over for that *tête–*

à–tête you mentioned."

She held up her hand, her cheeks red as she tried to speak, but no words came out. Then she put her hand to her forehead and groaned.

"I need coffee." And with those words, she turned around and headed to the kitchen.

Elsa sat looking up at him. Jarrod went on his haunches and let the dog smell his hand before he stroked her soft fur. "Well, baby girl, she was a little touchy. Looks like she may be supporting a hangover, huh?"

He had seen the bottle of wine and a single glass, both of them empty. He frowned. Although he completely understood how a person could take to drinking, considering what she'd been through, he hoped that wasn't the case here.

Standing, Jarrod went into the kitchen, where she was leaning one hip against the small counter. She turned her head as he walked in. "I'm sorry for being such an idiot, but you kissed me, and it's like you kissed all the rational thoughts from my head."

Her honesty amused him. "Did you enjoy it?"

"Yes."

"And that's a problem because…"

"Because I'm not supposed to enjoy it. I shouldn't, I don't want to experience it."

"Why?"

Maisy didn't answer and turned back to the coffee machine as it bleeped. Taking two mugs from the only wall cupboard, she poured some coffee into both of them, and handed one to him. Pushing the sugar canister toward him, she reached into the fridge, poured some milk into hers, and gave it to him for his.

He hated to see the look of despair in her eyes; it

clutched at his abdomen.

She didn't wait for him as she took her coffee and went out to the porch. He added sugar and milk to his mug and followed her outside, finding her leaning against the railings, cradling the cup as the breeze ruffled her paint-covered hair.

"I love this place," she said as he stood beside her. "Beth and Tom would have been happy here."

He brought the steaming coffee cup to his lips and blew before taking a sip. He could only imagine the pain she must be feeling, but then again, he really couldn't, because he'd never experienced that kind of pain.

"I feel so guilty for being here without them, and when I laugh, I remember I shouldn't. When, for a second, they are not in my thoughts, I am beside myself that I'm going to forget them. And when you…kissed me, I…I feel I'm betraying them by enjoying it."

He'd known Maisy felt like that. The minute she'd pulled away from him he could see it in her eyes.

"You shouldn't feel guilty for any of those things. Just because you find you can smile again doesn't suggest you're going to forget them. Do you think they don't know their mom loved them for one moment?" He lifted her down-bent head by the chin. "Maisy, you're allowed to move on. You have to live your life, and doing that isn't being disrespectful. It doesn't mean you'll forget them—it means that life goes on."

"I'm so scared I'm not going to remember what they look like," she whispered.

"Baby, you will never forget. That's just not possible. There will always be something that reminds you of one or the other."

"How did you get to be so wise? If I remember

correctly, the Jarrod I knew hated everyone and everything."

"I never hated you."

"Humph. You forgot me." She laughed.

"No, Maisy, I didn't."

"Yeah, yeah. Sure." She put her hand on his arm. "Thanks."

"For what?"

"For being here with me."

"How's the headache?" he asked, seeing her frown.

Maisy groaned. "Remind me never to drink a whole bottle of wine alone." She reached up to her forehead, smoothing the skin with her fingers. "There seems to be an army of dwarfs inside my head—with pickaxes."

"Why don't you go have a hot shower and take some aspirin, and you might feel more like a human being. I'll go do some measuring in the kitchen."

"Are you sure you don't need to return to your real job?"

"No, I'm due some time off, and my boss is very easy-going."

Her ex-husband had lied to her, and now Jarrod had disappointed himself by doing the same. He should have told her the truth. He should have come right out and said he owned the business. He cursed himself for putting on the t-shirt. It had just been natural to do when he knew he would be working. Why he'd lied, he had no idea. Perhaps he'd wanted to feel the way he had fifteen years ago.

Jarrod looked at her as she tipped back her cup to drink the last of her coffee. Her skin seemed almost luminescent in the early morning light, if not a little pale. She had a long neck, and the skin looked so soft it made him swallow with a little gulp as he realized he was getting aroused just watching her. Quickly, he looked back up; he noticed the green paint in her hair and grinned.

"What are you smiling at?"

"You."

"Why?"

He reached across and rubbed the strands between his finger and thumb. It was set, hard. "I pretty much don't think that's going to come out now."

She sighed then laughed. "It's oil paint, so I believe you're right. Aww well, I'll look like a punk." She spoke with a small smile as if she remembered why she had the paint in her hair in the first place.

"It's not too bad. At least your hair is short, and the blonde far outweighs the green."

"Yeah, and that makes me feel better!" She laughed again.

He took the cup from her. "Go on. I'm going to take a look at what work needs doing." She looked as though she wanted to argue for a moment, but he nudged her to go through the door. "Go."

He watched her leave, and lifting his coffee cup, he swallowed the remains. Elsa followed behind her, the do was her best friend where two hearts ached for the same thing. It tore at his insides how one person could endure so much pain. Jarrod couldn't imagine how she even got through the day. How did someone survive that kind of heartache? From now on he would make sure he was there for her.

Like a bolt, the realization came to him. She was what he'd been waiting for. It sounded crazy. Hell, it stood in the realms of senseless. He thought how oddly human emotions worked. Jarrod had never been short on girlfriends, and he used the word lightly because he never really had the time to spend with one girl.

But one touch, one breath... The awareness of feeling another person's emotions, their pain, and knowing that you cared more about how they were coping than how you felt. It completely overpowered what you perceived as a life you thought you had.

It was then realizing that your life would never be the same again. Jarrod didn't understand how it was possible to feel this way. His heart thumped inside his chest whenever he stood next to her, and one thing was certain—he wouldn't be going anywhere until he understood it.

****

Maisy let the hot water stream over her bent head, trying to eject those little hammers pounding away inside her brain. The heat felt good on her skin, the momentary pleasure allowing her to think of something other than how sad she felt.

Her mind wandered to Jarrod, as it had a lot in the last few days. Why would he want to help her with the home improvements? There was no denying the work needed doing, and she had kind of pushed it to one side. Perhaps doing this would help her to move on further.

Maisy remembered how it felt to have strong arms around her, and suddenly the water was far too hot, and she turned it to cold. He certainly knew how to kiss. Boy, did he know how? He brought back feelings in body parts she'd forgotten she had. It was damn bad manners on his part, especially after what she'd told him.

He had kissed her once. No, twice. And it completely overwhelmed her. Jarrod's offer of waiting for her to have a shower, so she could look at the world in a marginally civilized light, made her thankful, because she felt like shit.

Turning the shower off, she toweled herself dry then wrapped the downy softness around her. Her head was still pounding, so she took some aspirin from the wall cabinet, filled the empty glass on the sink with some water, and took them. She opened the bathroom door and looked both ways before stepping out of the room. With just one foot over the threshold, she nearly dropped her covering as Jarrod's voice stopped her in her tracks.

"Did the shower do the trick?"

"Yes, thank you." Was her voice always this breathy?

Jarrod took one step toward her, his tallness making her small hallway seem even tinier as he stood in between the bathroom and her bedroom. She had to look up, only to see his gaze drop from her face to the small gap that showed her skin, because she'd picked up the smallest towel.

Maisy felt her face redden, the heat spreading across her décolleté with a speed that embarrassed her, because she wasn't at an age where that should be happening.

"You look less…" Jarrod reached up and tweaked her still painted hair. "…disheveled. I think I like the green. It suits you."

"Liar." She'd made a complete fool of herself. "I'm sorry you had to see me like that. I promise I don't drink like that all the time."

The sun that shined through her bedroom window fell on his dark blond hair, streaking it with a golden hue, and she had the most irresistible urge to reach up and run her fingers through it. He had a square jaw, and at this angle his features were hawk-like; masculine but beautiful

He looked back at her. "Are you sorry about the kiss as well?"

She had dreamt about that kiss, but her inner emotions told her she couldn't ever expect to be happy. How could she live an everyday life after what had happened? The thought of moving on was unbearable and frightening. Her children had been her life.

However, looking at him now, she wasn't sure he fully understood how she felt. And why should he? The problem existed in her life, not his.

Maisy was afraid to admit that when they kissed she could quite easily have spontaneously combusted at the thought of his lips on hers. When she remained silent it was because, honestly, she didn't know how to reply.

Jarrod moved a little closer, his thumb and forefinger holding her chin as the pads smoothed at her still damp skin. His closeness invaded her senses. The smell of his soap or shower gel, whatever it was, titillated her faculty to perfect distraction. It was deliciously addictive.

"I don't want to talk about it," she whispered.

"It would be better to talk. It never does anyone any good to hold sadness inside them."

Yesterday afternoon he'd walked away, and she hoped he would do the same now. She waited for him to carry on.

God, did he know how utterly sexy he was? Why did she torture herself this way? She should walk away. But she didn't, it seemed her feet were rooted to the spot.

"But I understand, all that kissing might have been in poor taste in light of what you'd told me."

Holy cow, did he think that? It had been erotic, sensual. Even now as she thought about it she felt the need to cross her legs as the butterflies fluttered low down in her stomach.

Maisy was lying to herself if she thought his kiss meant nothing. She watched his mouth slowly curve as if he could read her mind, damn him.

"So, no interest in me at all? Didn't you feel the chemistry between us?"

He dipped his head, and she could feel his breath on her warm cheek. Her damn nipples suddenly became harder than they ever had before.

"Do you still think there is nothing between us?"

Maisy should have moved away as far as possible. But instead of stepping back, she tilted her head closer, bringing her in to meet his already descending lips. She shivered and pressed herself against him without one ounce of willpower to walk away. She had one hand fisted in his t-shirt while the other frantically kept hold of her towel.

"What the hell?" she whispered as his lips touched hers.

His eyes closed as hers fluttered the same way. Beneath her hand, his body felt warm and hard, and she couldn't help but tighten her grip.

"You don't want to do this with me," she said as he parted a little, both of them breathing heavily. "I have many problems in my life at the moment."

"Like what? You drank too much wine. We all do those things."

"No," she breathed out as her lips tingled from the warmth of his. She tried to search her very mushy brain for something that would ultimately put him off her. "I'm thirty-one, divorced, and trying to come to terms of the loss of my children. Isn't that enough?"

He shook his head.

"I get up to paint all hours of the night. If I drink red wine, I get drunk after two glasses, sing " *I'm a Believer* from *Shrek* and cry." There. If that still didn't put him off, she had one more thing, and she blurted out the words she never thought she'd say. "And I could win any farting competition hands-down in my college days." There. That would totally put him off.

He roared with laughter, and she blushed from the roots of her hair to her curling toes.

"Wow, that's a great achievement. I'm so thankful we don't have any attraction between us."

She could see by the tilt of his mouth he was teasing, but when she met his eyes they were full of something else, and it wasn't wittiness. It was evident she hadn't scared him off one iota, not even a dent in that thing he'd called chemistry.

Chapter 4

Maisy ran her fingers through her damp hair as she looked in the mirror. It stuck up in a way she didn't mind. She'd pulled on a pair of jeans and a tank top. Her skin appeared golden hue from the sun, but she was still too thin.

Swiping some chapstick across her dry lips, she breathed in deeply and turned to go find Jarrod. He was in the kitchen with a tape measurer, pencil, and paper on the floor beside him as he bent down to measure the room's length. It was a small kitchen made even smaller by his side.

Maisy tried not to stare, but that wasn't happening, because she couldn't stop looking at his mouth and remembering the feeling of those lips on hers. It gave her ideas about things she hadn't thought about in a very long time. A faint smile hinted around the corners of his mouth, and she looked up into amused eyes.

"So what do you have in mind?" he asked.

"What?" she said, feeling her face go hot.

"The kitchen?" he asked with a mischievous twinkle in his eye.

"Oh, yes," she said with relief, glad he couldn't read her mind. "Are you sure you have time for this?"

He nodded. "Don't worry about me. I have plenty of time to help you out."

"I don't know." Maisy hadn't thought about what

she wanted. "How about you surprise me? I'm not much of a cook anymore, and all I want is a few cupboards, perhaps some new flooring."

Jarrod nodded. "A blank canvas, my favorite kind." He smiled at her.

Why was her heart beating so hard? This guy made her feel things that she'd never felt before. She had a tingly flutter inside her belly something else she couldn't define. But it shouldn't be like that. She couldn't be happy. How could she bury her children and smile again? How could she do that? In what lifetime was that even possible?

Jarrod stood up and moved in front of her. His fingers tilted her chin, and she looked up into concerned eyes.

"Where were you?" he said. "You were somewhere that saddened you."

She allowed their eyes to meet for a split second and caught her breath. All too aware of the closeness between them, Maisy moved away to the living room, hoping to gain some distance, but Jarrod followed her closely.

She reached up and brushed her short hair back from her forehead and while doing so, caught him looking at the scar just above her right brow. It had faded somewhat but was still noticeable.

Before she could smooth her hair back down, he was in front of her. Very gently, so softly it almost broke something inside her, his fingertips caressed the rough skin. He didn't say anything, but the muscles in his jaw clenched several times.

"What happened?" he finally asked.

"The accident."

Tension seemed to grip his whole body, and after

51

another agonizing beat of her heart, he stepped away, allowing her to pull her hair back down.

When Elsa came through the storm door, letting it bang loudly behind her, Maisy jumped. The dog came and sat by her feet. She smoothed her hand down the dog's back, much to Elsa's pleasure. Maisy felt tears well up when Elsa slowly walked over to Jarrod and sat, looking up at him, her large brown eyes asking for some love.

Jarrod immediately went down on his haunches and petted the dog. The moment was so poignant she had to turn away. Elsa seemed to be coming to terms with the loss; until this day, Maisy thought Elsa would never come out of the depths of despair.

"Seems like I'm her friend now?"

Maisy turned back and smiled. "I'm glad." And she was, so much more than he would ever know, because it meant Elsa was finally learning to love without their little family. Maisy felt sad. She told herself she shouldn't be, because that's what she wanted, for Elsa to be happy.

"When do you want me to start in the kitchen?" Jarrod asked.

"It's entirely up to you."

"Okay, I'll do some final measuring and put an order in for the cabinets to be made. That leaves me clear to start on the floor before they're ready."

"That's great. I appreciate it." It was more than she expected. She had the money. That wasn't a problem. She'd used a lot of the money from the sale of her house in the UK to buy this one, but she still had a little nest egg left.

"No problem. Do you have any idea what kind of

pine you'd like to use?"

She looked at him and frowned. "There are different kinds?"

His mouth twitched. "Yes."

"You decide." She laughed. "I have not the slightest clue about one pine, let alone different kinds."

"So, if I get started tomorrow, that's okay with you?"

"Certainly."

They stood there for an awkward moment. Well, she felt uncomfortable, but he looked completely at ease. Maisy narrowed her eyes as her headache started pounding.

"Hangovers are a bitch," he said.

Maisy forced down a sick feeling. "They are, I'd forgotten how much." She brought her fingers up to her temples as she walked to the front door and opened it. "Fresh air, I think." She turned to go outside onto the porch.

The air from the water was warm, but Maisy's skin prickled with goosebumps, which in the heat of the day was silly. But she was well aware that it had nothing to do with temperature, and more to do with the man who'd come to stand beside her. They both looked at the deep blue Atlantic Ocean for a moment. The sound of the water breaking against the golden sands of Nags Head put you into a mesmeric mood.

"When you left all those years ago, I always kept a small seed of regret in my heart."

She turned to him and blinked with confusion. "Regret?"

He nodded. "I always wanted to kiss you but couldn't pluck up the courage."

"I'll let you in on a secret—I wanted you to kiss me."

He looked surprised. "You did? You always seemed so…so sisterly. You never showed any signs."

"I was a fifteen-year-old girl and shy. And you…you were this Adonis with your blond-streaked hair and green eyes."

He laughed. "I was wild. And you thought that?"

She nodded.

"Damn! I wish I'd known."

Running her tongue over her dry lips, she told him, "I thought a lot about you once I went home."

He reached over and tucked a short strand of hair behind her ear. "I thought about your hair flying behind you as you moved like lightning into the waves. It was a beautiful sight. "

Maisy frowned. She wanted to be honest with him. "I have no idea if I'm ready for anything like this, like us. I'm not a great gamble right now."

He stepped closer. "You've already told me that."

This man knew exactly how to comfort her, to make her feel safe. Almost as if he couldn't resist.

He dipped his head and kissed her.

This wasn't good. Well, it was good, but it wasn't going to end well.

"Jarrod," she whispered against his mouth.

"Hmm?" he murmured as he took her lips on an emotional journey that made her heartbeat and her nipples tingle. "Did I mention how much I love this short hair?" He cupped the back of her head with his large hand and threaded his fingers through the strands.

Holy cow. Her knees wobbled. She reached up to put her arms around his neck as he settled his fingers on her hips and drew her closer. Who was she kidding? They had an attraction all right. Her usually quiet dog came out through the door and sat close by, barking. She put her hand down to pat her, then resumed her grip on Jarrod's neck.

"Down, Elsa. It's okay," she said as the dog jumped up.

Jarrod looked down at Maisy with a smirk on his face. It was evident he knew what she was thinking.

"I thought we didn't have chemistry?" Jarrod said with a grin.

She let her eyes close briefly before looking back to his. "Okay, there is something there," she admitted begrudgingly.

"Just a little thing or a supersized one?" An amused smile played on his lips.

"Supersized. But," she added when his smile turned smug, "I haven't spent time with a man for a long time."

"So, what shall we do?"

She frowned. "What do you mean?"

"Do you want to go slowly, or have mad, passionate sex right here?" There was a playful tone in his voice, but she didn't feel like being teased, so she took two steps back from him.

They stood looking at each other, and she could feel annoyance traveling through her body at his suggestion. "I don't do casual sex."

"I didn't think you did." He arched his eyebrow. "Sorry, I was teasing. Don't you miss it?"

"I've never had casual sex."

"No, I mean sex in general."

"Not at all."

He shot her a surprised look. "Not even a tiny bit?"

"It never really meant that much to me." This conversation was becoming entirely too embarrassing.

"Then, honey, you've been doing it all wrong."

She felt the suggestion in the stance of his body, and she had no doubt whatsoever that whoever had sex with this man, they wouldn't forget it in a hurry. She looked up into his eyes when he put his fingers beneath her chin.

"Where were you?" he asked.

She couldn't stop the warm flush that spread across her cheeks, and throughout her body. Although his face was serious, his eyes were laughing.

He tweaked the lobe of her ear. "Come to dinner tonight?"

"I don't know. I have Elsa."

"Bring her with you."

"But I—"

"Just pasta, nothing else." He smiled. "It's just a meal."

She could do that. It would be nice to share a meal with someone else rather than eat on her own. "I would love to, thank you."

****

Jarrod spent the rest of the day with a smile on his face. As the sun dipped low in the dusky sky, he grabbed the bottle of red wine and opened it so it could breathe. Looking out at the now familiar view, he smiled at the thought of how much his life had changed in two days. It was crazy to think of the connection he had with Maisy.

His bachelorhood had been bugging him for some time. Yes, there were plenty of women, some good friends. But that thrill he'd gotten when he'd realized who Maisy was had hit him squarely in the solar plexus.

Jarrod remembered her laugh even after all the years that had passed. He used to pick her up and throw her in the waves. He remembered how hard his heart used to beat, but he had been too shy to say anything

He couldn't remember the last time he'd felt as nervous as he was feeling now. He walked outside and leaned against the railing, waiting and watching for her to appear in the distance.

Jarrod saw Elsa first, and she came straight up to him, wagging her tail. He went on his haunches and stroked the dog's head. "Where is she, girl?"

The dog barked, and he stood as Maisy's voice reached his ears.

"Seems Elsa couldn't wait to reach you." Maisy came up the steps and along the decking. "I see you've made a friend of her."

"It's mutual," Jarrod muttered. The tears he saw in Maisy's eyes went straight to his heart, for the dog and owner who had lost so much.

She handed him a bottle of wine.

"You didn't have to bring anything."

"Yes, I did."

"Come on." He ushered her into the kitchen through the open doors that led from the decking area.

"This is lovely," she said.

Jarrod surveyed her as her fingers smoothed along the black marble countertop. He had crafted the yellow pine cabinets and finished them with antique gold handles. It had taken him months to locate those handles, and he'd eventually found them in a house his company had been renovating.

He watched as she glanced around to the living room, at his comfortable sofas and the overflowing bookshelves.

"This is such a cozy room," she said of his open floor plan.

"If I come here in winter, it's lovely with the woodstove burning." Jarrod gestured to the vast space against the farthest wall where an old-fashioned Franklin stove sat surrounded by already cut logs.

"It looks great, Jarrod. You did this all by yourself?" She turned back and looked at him.

He nodded. "What can I get you to drink?" he asked.

"What have you got?"

"Coffee, water, soda, beer, and wine, red and white."

"Red wine sounds great, thanks." She smiled at him.

Maisy came over and peered at what he was cooking. It wasn't the first time his heart rate sped up a little at her closeness, and he swallowed heavily. She smelled of coconuts and warm, fresh air, and he had to stop himself from inhaling the scent at the curve of her slim, bare neck.

"I'm not a good cook," he said, trying to take his mind off what he wanted to do. "However, even I can cook spaghetti, garlic bread, and go to the store to buy ice cream for dessert."

"Sounds like my cup of tea."

He handed her the glass of wine he'd poured and frowned. "Cup of tea? Did you want tea?"

She laughed. "No. It's an English expression that means it's just what you want."

He chuckled. "Ah, yes." He noticed the slight flush along her cheekbones.

"We Brits are full of funny sayings like that." She took a sip of her wine before placing it on the countertop.

Jarrod picked up the glass and took her hand, leading her to one of the high stools on the other side of the counter from where he worked. "Sit," he instructed. "You're my guest."

"That doesn't mean I can't help."

"That's exactly what it means."

"If you insist." She sighed.

"I do."

"Bossy thing, aren't you?" Her tone suggested she was teasing him.

"Oh, you have no idea." He winked at her, and she laughed.

"No, and perhaps it's better if I don't."

He looked over her shoulder and chuckled. "I think someone has made themselves comfortable."

She turned around and followed his gaze. "Elsa, get off the sofa."

"No, it's fine. I don't mind," Jarrod said, looking at the dog fully stretched out on the cushions.

"Are you sure? That sofa looks kinda expensive."

"I'm sure. Elsa looks way too relaxed for me even to try."

"She does. I've never known her to be so at ease. Not since the accident."

"I was hoping the owner would feel the same way?"

She looked at where he still held her hand and then directly at him. "Yes. Yes, she does."

"Good," he said before letting go and returning to onion chopping. "So, how's your day been?"

"Nothing exciting. I cleaned a little, read, and took Elsa for a long walk. How about you?"

"I ordered the supplies I needed to start working on your kitchen."

"Do you want me to pay you now?"

"No. Jarrod didn't want her to pay, he was doing it for his pleasure and hers as well, and he didn't want to discuss it. "There's plenty of time to sort that out."

"Okay, you let me know when you need it."

Jarrod nodded, but as far as he was concerned, that day would never come. He would enjoy this project. It beat the boardroom, and he was the boss, so he could take a few weeks off work if he wanted. He went to the large, double refrigerator and got the garlic butter.

"Is this okay for you?" he asked. "Or would you prefer cheese on the bread?"

"Garlic butter is great."

Jarrod smiled before slicing the French loaf in half and spreading both sides generously with the aromatic butter, then he placed them on a tray and put it in the oven. He had worried things might be a little strained, but he couldn't remember ever feeling quite so relaxed.

"I love all the pine. Is this what I'm having?"

"No, yours is going to be lighter. Your house is quite a bit smaller, so we don't want to darken the rooms. I've chosen a more beachy look, you'll see," he said. "Are you regretting giving me free rein?"

"Absolutely not. I'm excited to see what you're going to do, and I honestly didn't realize there were so many different types of wood available."

"Most people don't, but I love working with the varied grains and colors. No one piece ever looks the same."

Jarrod observed her as she sat in his kitchen. She was so beautiful—not just what you could see, but on the inside too.

"What are you thinking?" she asked him.

"That it's nice having you here." Jarrod reached across the counter and took her hand.

"Thank you for asking me." She smiled, her voice a whisper mixed with the sound of the waves through the open windows.

It wasn't the first time her voice had left a tingling up and down his spine. Even all those years ago he had felt it, but he'd been too scared to do anything about it. But now he was acutely aware of the chemistry between them, and he intended to do something about it this time.

"It's my pleasure," he said simply, because it was. "Do you think that you will ever be happy again?" He asked the question because he wanted to know if it was possible to live your life after such tragedy.

"I love my children just as much as if they were here now, the only difference is they now live in heaven. There is no 'moving on' or 'getting over it'. I wish there was a box where I could find a solution to my pain, but there is no elixir. The grief will always be with me, the gap in my life will never be filled, and the empty space of missing children lasts a lifetime. Because I have clawed my way from the depths of despair, when joy comes..." She smiled at him. "I've learned to be forever grateful when it does. So, in answer to your question..." She shrugged her shoulders. "Truthfully, I hope so, but there is nothing, and I mean nothing, I take for granted. I have learned to live life this way, and it gives me joy to be able to do this."

He nodded. "You're such a special person, do you know that?"

"No, I'm not, and don't have any illusions about me, I'm just a woman trying to survive."

He guessed it was an argument he wasn't going to

win. Perhaps one day he would make her feel differently. "So, what is the plan? Are you going to stay here forever?"

"Gosh. Forever is a long time, and one thing I have learned is that nothing in life is guaranteed." Maisy twisted the stem of the glass in between the fingers of both hands. "I take each day as it comes."

"I'm sorry you've experienced so much pain."

"Life happens. It's a bitch sometimes, but once it's made up its mind, there's no changing it."

Jarrod knew she was scant with the truth, so he didn't push it.

"What about you, Jarrod? Are you happy?"

Jarrod thought about his life and what he'd achieved. He was happy enough. He smiled at her. "I have nothing to complain about."

However, there was nothing wrong with hope, and he wanted Maisy to become a lot more involved with his life. Even all those years ago they'd had a connection. But Jarrod had been way too immature to realize what he felt could be something more.

****

Maisy studied the man standing in front of the stove. She felt happy, and hadn't in such a long time. The sun had started to set, but it still shone into his home. His blond-streaked hair, more contained than it used to be when he was younger, was now cut short. But it looked as silky as she remembered. His skin was tanned, and he had a slight growth of beard on his jaw which made him exude sexiness.

Jarrod's hands had strength and shape—worker's hands. His movements were deft and efficient. As Maisy watched him, she felt the subtle change in her awareness of this man. A memory returned of her feelings for him all those years ago as a teenager, desperate to feel his lips on hers. And yet she never had.

Jarrod seemed proficient at what he was doing and worked diligently to prepare their meal.

"Come with me," he said, picking up her glass of wine and his own. "Let's sit outside while the food finishes cooking. The sunset is spectacular from here."

Maisy stood and followed, sitting on the love bench beside him, facing the Atlantic Ocean. She was aware of the warm sun on her face and the scent of salt from the water as the waves crashed onto the pale golden sand.

People were still milling about, but not as many as earlier. Maisy slipped her flip-flops off and curled her feet beneath her. Elsa came and plopped down beside her on the decking floor.

"What are you thinking?" Jarrod asked.

She took a sip of her wine before putting it down on the small table at her right.

"I'm thinking how lucky I am to be sitting here." She wished with everything she had that her children were there with her. They would have loved the beach so much.

Jarrod reached across and took her hand. She admitted to herself it was a pleasant experience that sent a prickle of excitement up her arm.

"I love having you here," he said, looking at her.

There it was again, that sense of contentment and excitement every time he spoke to her. His voice caressed her emotions, always sensitive and full of warmth—and that very sexy undertone that was always there.

"Why have you never married?" she asked.

"I've never met anyone that made me want to give up my freedom."

"You're happy with the work you do?"

"Yes. I've always loved working with wood. I used to carve little wooden animals and sell them at the markets."

"Very entrepreneurial. Do you still do it?"

"Yes."

"I'd love to see them."

"Perhaps later?"

"That would be lovely."

When she'd been on holiday with her parents, she admired him when he'd been out on the water surfing. His devil-may-care attitude had been so evident then; it had been clear he hadn't a care in the world for his safety.

He still held her hand, and his thumb rubbed rhythmically on the inside of her wrist. Her heartbeat had increased, and she became very aware of how he was looking at her.

"What would you need now to make you happy?" he asked.

Maisy looked at him, not feeling at all uncomfortable at his focused gaze on her. "That's why I came here—to help me work out what's next in my life."

"You're so courageous. You know that, right?"

"What makes you say that?" she asked, puzzled.

"So many people would have given up, wouldn't have been able to cope with the loss. When you told me, my heart ached for you."

"I almost did."

"What? Give up?"

She nodded. "It was very rough for so long afterward. I'd lost everything. My children were my life.

I gave birth to them, and they were as much a part of me as my body was, if not more so. Afterward, when they were gone..." She swallowed back the bile threatening to rise. Tears were always never very far away. Even now when she talked about Tom and Beth tears threatened to spill from her eyes, but she held them back. Jarrod squeezed her hand as she looked at him. "It was so hard, it still is." She dropped her shoulders as she stared out into the ocean's vastness. The glow across the sky reminded her of a palette of orange paint in different shades.

"I can't imagine what you must have gone through," he said.

The emotion in his voice touched Maisy. Jarrod's words were softly spoken but firm enough for her to take note. He was such a big man, but quite clearly he had a big heart, and she almost forgot they weren't more than friends.

"Thank you."

"I didn't mean for you to get upset."

"I'd love to say I wasn't." Maisy gave a long sigh. "But whenever I think of them I'm always going to be like this."

"Do you remember when I tried to teach you to surf?"

Giggling, she nodded. "Do I ever, it seemed to take forever to learn to stay on that board."

"You were so stubborn and determined. It didn't matter how often you fell in the water, you kept getting back on, until you stopped drinking half the Atlantic Ocean."

She laughed, glad to lighten the mood. "I got dunked so many times. I was in the water more often than not."

He flashed her one of those addictive grins. "But you conquered it. I remember watching you surf your first wave. I'll never forget the sound of your laughter."

"I'd like to say I enjoyed it, but I didn't." She giggled at his expression. "I'm sorry, I just didn't."

"Stop talking, woman. Those words don't even register with me."

"We're not those teenagers anymore." She spoke while looking out at the water.

"No, we're not."

His tone made her turn back to him. The intensity she saw in his eyes took her back fifteen years. Although now she recognized it as passion, she hadn't known what it was all those years ago.

"What would you do differently if we were still those young individuals?" she asked him, suspecting she already knew the answer.

"I would have been braver and kissed you."

"You say that now because you're no longer that teenage boy," she teased him.

"Perhaps, but you make me feel like I am one."

The air between them was positively spine-tingling.

"I've never felt as relaxed with another woman as I do with you."

"Jarrod…"

He looked a little embarrassed, which surprised her. He stood. "I think it's time we ate."

She got up and followed him back into the kitchen. Maisy didn't know what to make of what he'd said, and she didn't want to think about it. She wasn't ready for anything more than friendship. That was all she could give.

****

The meal was delicious. Maisy couldn't remember the last time she'd eaten so much.

"Would you like to go for a walk? Jarrod asked.

Maisy hesitated, not sure if she should go home.

"It's okay if you don't want to," he said tenderly.

"It's not that. I don't know if I'm—"

"Believe me, I know, and I understand. I would never push you into something you're not comfortable doing. Just a short walk, nothing else." He extended his hand to take hers. "Come with me."

For a second she paused, trying to think of a way to say no. She couldn't so she placed her hand inside his, and he gripped her fingers gently. She did the same and swallowed back the emotion she felt.

Elsa followed them as they took the steps down. Still in her bare feet, Maisy enjoyed the feeling of the cooling sand, her toes sinking through the grains. Being together on this beach brought back memories of their short time together.

The tide was out so they strolled almost to the water's edge. Jarrod let go of her hand to bend down and pick up a pebble. He skimmed it along the water, completely missing the waves, and they watched it bounce along as if it was flying through the air.

Maisy picked up a small piece of driftwood and threw it for Elsa. She chased after it, picked it up, and headed back toward them. Maisy couldn't help but notice that Elsa seemed to be running slower. She had gained some weight, which was odd because Maisy walked her daily. Perhaps she needed to cut down her snacks a little. Maisy liked to give her treats. Too many it would seem

Elsa stopped in front of Jarrod and stared up at him

with expectant eyes. He took the wood from her and threw it down the beach, and she ran after it.

Maisy smiled. "It looks like you have a friend for life."

She laughed at the sight of the gentle breeze blowing at Elsa's floppy ears as she sped after the wood. It made her heart lurch to see her running like that. It had seemed the poor dog had been unhappy for so long; it brought back memories of how much she used to play with the children.

"I remember the summer we became friends. Although your parents kept such a wonderful eye on you, it was hard to get alone time. I don't think they liked me," Jarrod said.

"It wasn't that they didn't like you. I think Mum and Dad were a little worried about their daughter hanging around with a beach bum." She chuckled at his expression.

"Well, I suppose I did look a little like that." He grinned. "But I would have treated you right."

"I know."

"Do you think you might have more kids someday?" he asked her.

She felt a heavy weight against her heart at the thought. "I'm too old to think of starting all over again."

"I guess you are an old lady." He said it playfully.

She pushed at his arm teasingly. "Hey, less of the 'old', please."

When his arm tightened around her, Jarrod's scent permeated her nose. The smell of his soap was lemons shrouded with a hint of musk.

"Do you ever think about it?" he asked.

"I have once or twice. But how could I be a good

mum? I would wrap them up in cotton wool, afraid to let them out of my sight."

"Statistically, it wouldn't happen again."

"How do you know that? How can anyone be sure it wouldn't happen again?"

"What happened to you was awful but also rare. The chances of it occurring to the same person again would be almost impossible." He spoke softly, and she had to lean in closer to hear him against the background noise of the waves as they came onto the sand.

"I don't know, Jarrod. It's so terrifying."

"Yeah, I get that. But I think maybe you're moving on from the sadness to the happy memories, and now you get to live your life again. The worst is behind you."

Her mind soaked up what he'd said, and she had to admit she hadn't thought of it like that. "I hope you're right."

For a moment, they looked at each other. It was dark now that the sun had set, but she could see his eyes by the full moon's light.

"Hey, do you remember what we used to do?" Jarrod led her away from the water and beckoned for her to lie next to him. "Come on."

"Jeez, Jarrod." She giggled. "I haven't been stargazing since I did it with you."

"Then I think it's time you reacquainted yourself to the perfect constellations we have here in North Carolina."

She laughed and lay down beside him. Elsa joined her with a deep sigh, and they both chuckled. As they settled back, Jarrod's hand again found hers, and she let him hold it.

"I had forgotten how beautiful it is," she said as she

looked up into the darkened sky with its sprinkling of shining stars, thousands of them, so clear, so bright.

"I love this place, and when I get the chance to spend some time here I take it."

"You're lucky your friend allows you to stay here whenever you want."

"Yes, I guess I am."

He spoke quietly. Maisy sensed something in his tone, but she couldn't quite put her finger on it.

He pointed to a constellation. Maisy twisted her head to look.

"Cassiopeia," he said.

"Gosh, yes, although I would have never remembered the name."

He brought her hand to his mouth and kissed it. Maisy swallowed hard as his lips sent shivers down her arm.

"Do you know which one that is?" he asked, indicating one part of the sky.

"How could I forget? Pisces."

"Yes, your birth sign. March tenth."

"Oh my God, you remember my birthday?"

"I do."

Maisy laughed while he continued resting his lips on the back of her hand. He turned it over and kissed the inside of her wrist.

"This is lovely," she said as she turned back to look at the sky.

"What about that one?" He pointed to her left.

"Capricornus—your birth sign, January fifteenth."

"Well done. I'm impressed you remembered."

Maisy turned her head to look at him. "You were a marvelous teacher." She reached out with her other hand

and touched his jaw. "You need a shave."

"Uh-huh. Do you mind?"

"No," she said as he leaned into her fingers and the raspiness of his bristles sent tingles down her spine. "Why are you asking if I mind?"

"Because." He turned onto his side and looked down at her. "I want to do this." He leaned into her neck and nuzzled the delicate skin.

She was breathless as his lips found the sensitive spot just behind her ear.

"This is nice." She spoke in a whisper as her breath staggered a little.

"You smell so good," he said. "And I've been dying to do this all night long."

Maisy tilted her head to one side so it would be easier. They were both breathing hard, and her heart rate seemed erratic at best. She smoothed her fingers through his hair, and it was as silky as she'd wondered earlier.

"Are you okay?" he asked as he lightly brushed his lips across hers.

"Yes. Yes, I'm all right." She took a deep breath and felt his mouth on the corner of hers.

"Maisy…"

"Jarrod, just kiss me."

Lying on the sand beneath the stars, they kissed, and she thought about how this was what it would have been like had they done it all those years ago. Only now they had more passion, more experience.

Jarrod kissed her as though she was the most precious thing in the world. Then he shifted so she lay beneath him. It lived up to everything she had dreamed of and more. The passion was slow and honest as he dotted kisses on her eyelids and face, and then her lips again.

"I didn't plan this," he said, looking down at her.

She caressed his jaw. "I'm enjoying it."

"Mmm, you are?" he said against her lips.

"I am." She felt an urgency in his touch.

But this should have been wrong. Maisy wasn't ready to be loved. She didn't deserve it.

However, the unbidden chemistry between them felt sumptuously electrifying. It should have surprised her, but it didn't, not one little bit. Feeling a little bold, Maisy slid her hands beneath his t-shirt and let her fingers smooth the skin on his back. She could feel the ripple of his muscles.

He shuddered and pushed his erection into the vee of her legs, and she couldn't help but widen them to accommodate him.

"God!" He groaned as he laid his forehead against hers. "I promised I wouldn't rush you, and I won't. But I want you so much. I have spent the last fifteen years waiting for you."

"Jarrod, I want you too. This isn't one-sided. I just don't think I can be so involved now."

He kissed her gently, a whisper of a touch with his warm lips. "Sweetheart, I know you're not ready, but I'm willing to wait as long as it takes."

"I'm sorry."

"Don't apologize, Maisy." He kissed her eyelids again, softly, sweetly. "We've got all the time in the world."

Maisy sighed, closing her eyes as contentment flowed through her body for the first time in so long. She let him comfort her. Maisy hadn't realized how much she needed this, whatever 'this' was. Nothing quite like that feeling of someone caring for you, being desired, and making your heart beat at twice its normal rate. She was still a woman, but hadn't felt like one in years—long before she'd lost her children.

"I can't promise you anything," she said as he trailed kisses along the dip in her top, just touching the small swell of her breasts. "You know I have this court case coming up."

"I know," he said, kissing her beneath her chin. "We'll take it slow, I promise."

Chapter 5

The shrill sound of her mobile phone woke Maisy the next morning. For a moment it startled her. Looking at her bedside clock, she was surprised to see it was past nine. She reached across and answered the noisy phone.

"Please don't tell me you're still in bed?" a teasing voice spoke into her ear.

"Okay, I won't," she replied.

"But you are," he guessed.

"Yes, I am. I can't remember the last time I slept past seven."

"Would the reason be that extra glass of wine you had?"

Maisy laughed. She lay back and stretched, grimacing a little at the old wound on her leg—a stealthy reminder of the accident in which her children had lost their lives. She let her head rest on the soft pillow and remembered the evening she'd spent with Jarrod.

"It might be."

"Hmm! Do you think you could get up and let me in?"

She could imagine that cocky smile as it lifted at the corners of his mouth.

"I have rather a lot of wood I've unloaded at the back door."

Shit! "Are you outside now?" She threw the covers back and jumped out of bed, much to Elsa's surprise.

74

Eagerness fluttered in her belly, and she placed her hand there, expecting to feel butterflies jumping around beneath her skin. Maisy instinctively felt a need to see him, but she wasn't sure what she thought.

She stood up and slipped on yoga pants over her panties. She picked up a t-shirt from the chair in the corner of the room and pulled it over her head.

Looking down at herself, Maisy groaned. "Oh my God, what a mess." She could only imagine how her hair looked as she opened the door to her bedroom and stepped out, almost losing her balance as Elsa brushed past her legs.

As she made her way through the living room toward the kitchen's back door, her eye caught the covered canvas. She stopped. What was she doing? She had no right to be happy like this when the two most precious people in her life were gone.

Bile rose in her throat and lifted her hand to her mouth as she swallowed back the bitter taste. The dead weight of the loss still squeezed at her heart in a grip so tight it took her breath away, and there was no room for happiness, not even her own.

What had she been thinking? She wasn't some horny teenager; she was a thirty-year-old woman, a mum who'd lost her children because she'd been too neglectful. Hadn't she known her ex-husband liked to drink? That's why she'd left him in the first place. He'd drunk a bottle of whiskey and hit her, but he never did it again, because she'd packed up herself and her children and left him.

Bloody hell, why hadn't she realized their father had been inebriated that day he'd picked them all up from school? Why, oh why? A sob escaped her lips. She stifled the noise.

Another knock sounded at the door. Elsa whined, almost crossing her legs, desperate to relieve herself. Maisy took a deep breath and continued to the kitchen where she unlocked the door. The poor dog shot out, passing Jarrod standing on the porch, hands on hips, looking at her with a frown marking his smooth forehead.

He took his time letting his gaze run over her, leaving her breathless as she stood there like an idiot. Elsa sniffed and peed on every corner, and Maisy wondered—as she had before—if she had an extended bladder.

Maisy turned back to Jarrod. A large toolbox set at his feet, and slung around his narrow hips was his toolbelt with an array of instruments.

Quickly, she averted her gaze from his crotch. She felt her cheeks heat up considerably when she caught him looking at her with a mischievous glint in his eyes. Damn him!

"You have lots of tools on your belt." Dear Lord! She almost groaned out loud when she heard the words come out of her mouth. She couldn't quite believe she'd said them.

"That's observant of you," he said, tongue in cheek.

"Don't be a smartass, Jarrod."

His silence unnerved her. "I wasn't being a smartass. You were the one staring at my crotch."

She gasped. "I was not." She stuck her hands in the pockets of her pants, and stared at him indignantly.

"Oops," he said. "I momentarily forgot it was my tools that had grabbed your attention."

"Damn you, Jarrod."

"Maisy Fields, you are a conundrum, making me like you even more."

"Why is that?"

"Because last night was beautiful…the stars, your kisses."

"And this morning I'm different?" She knew he was right. Last night had been lovely, but she still doubted her readiness for a relationship with this man.

He nodded. "Until your eyes wandered, and by the way, I don't mind that they did."

She squealed in embarrassment and put both hands on her cheeks, which were hot enough to fry eggs.

"See? A conundrum." Picking up his toolbox, he stepped inside, brushing past her. She followed him into the living room where he set his toolbox on the floor.

God damn it, but her eyes automatically strayed to his ass where his wrangler jeans stretched nicely across the toned shape, which meant that the resolve she'd had to keep her gaze averted from his mouth-watering body just blew up in her face.

Without turning around, he sat on his haunches as he opened the box.

"Ya know, if you stopped thinking about it so hard you wouldn't frighten yourself so much," Jarrod said.

"I'm not thinking about anything," she said, embarrassed at what she had been thinking.

"You're working so hard to convince yourself, yet you can't seem to take your eyes off my ass."

"Of all the egotistical, high-handed things to say, that takes the biscuit." As she spoke she grabbed the cushion from the sofa and threw it at him. He must have realized something was coming, because he turned just in time to catch it.

Jarrod laughed. "I do think the lady protests too much."

In a not-so-very grown-up way she stamped her foot before heading to the bathroom, where she banged the door loudly to the infuriating sound of him chuckling.

****

Jarrod started to move what little furniture she had onto the porch. He'd never met anyone like Maisy, and it was only now that he realized it. He'd never had any problem attracting the opposite sex. Even as a teenager the girls had liked him. And he'd always had the greatest respect for females. Jarrod loved their softness, adored the conversation, and up to now, he'd liked being single, so he could indulge in all those things.

He'd made reservations for tonight at the Fish Heads Bar and Grill. Nothing fancy, but they had a good selection of beers, and the food was excellent. He hoped Maisy still loved seafood. She used to. When they were teenagers they would go eat shrimp at Hurricane Mo's.

For the first time in his life, he doubted himself. He'd wanted to surprise Maisy by taking her out tonight. He thought it would be fun and wanted to spend more time with her.

Fuck! He'd never been indecisive. But with Maisy, Jarrod hesitated as to whether he was doing the right thing or not. As much as he'd enjoyed last night he didn't want to hurry her. She'd been through so much already. Maybe taking a few steps back would be wise? And give her some breathing space until at least after the court date.

He decided to go slower. Well, try to. When he was near Maisy, it seemed her succulent lips took precedence over any sensible thoughts he had. Jarrod always thought he wasn't an impulsive man, and he usually never made decisions lightly. Lots of thought went into all his choices.

However, Maisy…well, that quite literally threw all rational thought out the window. The minute he touched her, any resolve he had disappeared.

Once they had cleared the furniture out of the living room, Jarrod squatted down to give Elsa his full attention. He ruffled her fur. "Hey, baby girl."

His reward was a very wet and enthusiastic lick to his face, and he laughed.

"She's taken a real liking to you."

Jarrod looked up to see Maisy stepping toward them. The white halterneck top showed off her tan and cleavage, and he swallowed. Reservations and the decision to slow down only minutes before were already fading into the distant part of his memory.

A pair of faded, frayed denim shorts showed her slim, toned legs. Her blonde hair was damp from her shower, and the aroma of her coconut lotion impaled his senses. The memory of that scent as he'd trailed kisses along her collarbone the night before made his breath catch in his lungs.

God, he couldn't help but want her with every fiber of his being. *I like her too.* Jarrod shook his head as he remembered she'd spoken about Elsa.

He stood up, and they faced each other. Maisy was tiny compared to him, and she let her head fall back a little as she looked up at him. She slipped her hands into her shorts pockets, and he couldn't help but notice the action pushed her breasts together. Oh dear Lord! He felt the zipper of his jeans strain against his growing attraction toward her. Fucking hell!

"Right," he said, his voice low and gruff. "One more thing to come out, and then I can remove the flooring, readying for the new wood."

"Are you sure you have time? Just doing the kitchen is more than enough."

"I might as well do it, and then you can have the same flooring all the way through."

"Thank you, Jarrod. I appreciate you doing this for me. I hope you aren't going to get into trouble with your boss for undertaking this."

"I told you everything is fine."

Jarrod smiled, although he knew he should have told her the truth. He didn't want her to think he replicated her rich ex-husband in any way. But in trying to be different, he'd made himself the same by hiding his wealth.

"All we need to move out now is your easel and paints," he said.

A sudden look of horror filled her eyes, and she turned around and went over to the covered image. Jarrod watched her as she stood in front of it, and he desperately wanted to know what was hidden beneath the white sheet. She started to lift the easel, but he stepped forward and put his hand over hers. Her small fingers gripped it tightly, as if she was too frightened to let it go.

"It's okay, I won't look. Just tell me where to put it."

He could see the sadness in her expression. Her eyes filled with emotions he couldn't even begin to understand. It broke his heart to see her in so much distress. She bit down on her bottom lip to stop the trembling. Her chest heaved, and he wasn't sure she'd let go of the easel, until she nodded and drew her hands from beneath his.

"Can you put it in the bedroom?"

"Sure thing. You bring the paints." He carefully picked up the stand and carried it to her room. He set it down in the corner she indicated.

"Thank you for not asking me what was beneath the cover."

"No worries. I'm sure when you're ready you'll tell me. But if you don't, that's your call, and I respect your wishes."

He stood for a moment and watched as she straightened the sheet that had slipped off one corner.

"You know, Maisy, giving yourself permission to be happy is okay. No one is going to say you don't deserve it."

She smiled. "I know. But it's still hard for *me* to say I deserve it, because I don't think I do."

****

Jarrod started pulling up the old flooring. Maisy offered to help, but he wouldn't let her. So, leaving him a jug of iced tea, she took Elsa on her morning walk. As always, the sounds of children playing stopped Maisy in her tracks. She watched them with a smile on her face but a tug of pain in her heart.

God, how long would she have this pain? It never seemed to dissipate, although she liked to think she was coping better now than in the beginning. And she was.

The sound of the water crashing against the sand brought their voices nearer to her, chatting and giggling as they rolled around in the sand with great hilarity. They looked to be around the same age as her babies would have been.

Maisy closed her hands into fists, her nails digging into the skin, then she stretched them out, letting her fast breathing slow, and put into practice the pranayama breathing she had learned with her yoga. Inhaling to the count of ten, exhaling to number twenty, and slowly her heart rate reduced in speed. She managed to stop the anxiety attack before it controlled her. Damn! Just when she thought she was managing, something came along and knocked her for six.

"Hey, are you coming in for coffee?"

The sound of Dottie's voice—her friend of only a few months—made her turn around and wave.

"Elsa." She called the dog from the water's edge. Another dog she'd made friends with stood beside her; they'd been playmates right from her first walk on the beach.

Elsa came immediately. Trotting at Maisy's side, she followed her to the beach house Dottie shared with her husband, Mike, and their six-month-old baby, Sam. Dottie came down the steps from the second-floor balcony to meet her.

"You were out late last night?" her friend asked.

Maisy smiled at Dottie standing on the porch with her hands on her hips. The breeze lifted her long, dark hair away from her beautiful face, a teasing smile on her lips as she waited for Maisy to answer. She was not in the least bit surprised that Dottie knew.

"Go on, surprise me. How did you know I was out?"

"Because I was craving ice cream, I sent Mike to the store to get some."

"What time was that?"

"Around eleven, and when he passed, your place was in darkness."

"I could have been asleep."

Dottie raised her eyebrows. "Were you?"

"No, I wasn't…you missed your calling in life, you could have been a spy." Then it dawned on her what her friend had just said.

"You wanted ice cream at that time of night?" She looked down at Dottie's stomach and then back up at her face. "You're pregnant?"

Her friend nodded with a smile that said everything.

"Oh my God, that's fabulous news." She went over and hugged her friend, then stepped back to look into her eyes. "Are you happy?"

"Yes, I am. We both are. Sam will only be just over a year old when this little one is born." Dottie patted her stomach. "But that's the way it is." She shrugged. "It will be nice for them to be so close together rather than having a large age gap."

"Aww, Dottie, I'm delighted for you."

"Come on, let's go sit on the balcony. Sam's gone down for a nap."

She followed Dottie up the stairs to the balcony. Maisy closed the safety gate behind her and sat on the cushioned chair at the round, pine table, the parasol protecting them from the harsh sun. A large playpen in the corner also had a canopy to protect Sam while playing with his toys.

Maisy looked out at the ocean. "This is such a fantastic view you have here," she said, admiring all the different blues prevalent as the surf crashed against each other.

She felt Elsa sit beside her and automatically reached out to stroke her soft fur. The dog pushed into the caress.

"You knew I was coming?" Maisy took in the carafe of coffee and the small basket full of freshly baked blueberry muffins.

"Of course I knew. You do the same walk every day."

"My God, am I that predictable?" She laughed.

"Yes," Dottie replied in a teasing tone. "Did I tell you Mike and I got married here?"

Maisy shook her head. "No, you didn't. What a perfect place."

"Yes, it is, isn't it?" her friend said as she poured the coffee and passed a cup to Maisy.

"Thank you." She poured cream into the black liquid.

"I'll show you the pictures one day."

"I'd love that." She accepted one of the muffins from Dottie. "You baked these this morning?"

"Yes. I wanted Mike to have something fresh before he left for work."

Her husband had a string of hotels along the west coast, but his offices were based in Chesapeake. It was a two-hour drive one way, but because Dottie loved the beach house and didn't want to move, Mike made the drive every day without complaint.

When Maisy had first met Mike, he had charmed her, and she could see that he was besotted with his wife and their son. It always tugged at her heartstrings, remembering what it was like to have a child's love and to give it back unconditionally.

"So, where and what were you doing last night?"

Maisy told Dottie about Jarrod and how they'd met all those years ago and coincidentally again a few days back. "It's good. Being with Jarrod makes me feel things I haven't felt in a long time."

"Come on, elaborate on those, ah…feelings."

"Mmm! I have to say it was more than a little hot between us. I'm not sure if that's a good idea or not." Maisy broke a piece of her muffin, put the soft cake into her mouth, and then groaned loudly. "Oh. My. God. This is amazing."

Dottie laughed at her.

"No, really, these are delicious."

"Well, by the look on your face, girl…you seriously need to have an orgasm."

"Dottie!" Maisy squeaked. She could feel her cheeks flush with color, and she reached up and put her hands on her hot skin, almost choking as the cake went down the wrong way.

"Listen, Maisy. It's time you started to live your life. I won't even pretend to know the horror you have been through, but everyone deserves to be happy, even you. Although I know you have this preconceived idea, you don't." She reached across and put her hand over Maisy's resting on the table. "Let yourself enjoy. And don't overthink it."

Maisy looked surprised at her.

"It's in your eyes, honey."

"I feel guilty."

"Because of Beth and Tom?"

Maisy nodded.

"What was it like between you and your husband?"

Maisy thought for a moment. Right from the beginning, their marriage had been built on lies. She should have recognized Jack's family name; who didn't know of the Milords? They were an old family who had lived in a large mansion outside Chester, UK, for generations. But she hadn't, and it was too late when she'd found out about him and his money. She'd already fallen in love…she'd thought.

"It was okay, to begin with until I fell pregnant with Tom. I didn't know that Jack's family had money until after we got engaged. I quickly learned that his mummy and daddy were a large part of his life. They held the purse strings, and Jack was very money-oriented."

"So, you didn't know he had money?"

"No. Not to such an extent that he didn't have to work if he chose not to. Jack worked in finance. His family owned a large publishing house ."

"Did he lie about his wealth?" Dottie asked.

Maisy shook her head. "It wasn't his money, it was his parents." She was glad she had sunglasses on so Dottie couldn't see the pain she knew was in her eyes. "He drank, and I didn't realize how much until after we married. Finally, after the children were born, I decided enough was enough. He'd disappear for days at a time, the all-nighters and his bad temper when I questioned him about where he'd been."

Dottie reached over, laid her hand over hers, and clasped it.

"I should have smelled the alcohol on him that day, but he'd been on the wagon and had promised me he'd gotten it under control."

"Honey, don't do this to yourself. It's not your fault."

"His family has been fighting in the courts with the best lawyers, but it doesn't matter how long they drag it out. Jack was charged with involuntary manslaughter, and he should be sentenced in court at the end of the month. I don't have to go, but I will."

"He will get what he deserves."

"No, because it won't bring back my children, so

he'll never get what he deserves." Maisy gave her a sad smile. "I haven't known you long, but you are a good friend."

"Hey." Dottie patted her hand before removing it. "I have an ulterior motive."

Maisy chuckled, glad the mood had lightened. "You do?"

"Uh-huh."

"Spit it out then."

"Babysitting duties?"

"Anytime. I love looking after Sam. You know that."

"Saturday night?"

"It's a date." Maisy picked up her muffin and took another bite of the yummy sponge.

"So." Dottie tapped her short fingernails on the tabletop. "Have you and Jarrod done the deed yet?"

Maisy swallowed her mouthful the wrong way and started to cough as it got stuck in her throat. Dottie handed her a napkin. Maisy covered her mouth, her friend's amused expression very evident as Maisy took off her glasses, laying them on the table as she wiped her eyes.

"Jeez, I nearly choked to death."

"Umm, death by muffin. They are good, aren't they?"

"No, not because of that."

"I know," Dottie said, laughing. "You're such an innocent, Maisy."

"I'm never going to get this muffin eaten if you keep asking me questions like that. And I'm not innocent."

"How many men have you slept with?"

"One." Damn, Dottie was right. What knowledge

did she have of the opposite sex?

"I rest my case." Dottie folded her arms.

Maisy laughed.

"So…"

Maisy sighed, exasperated. "No."

"Why not?"

"Because I don't think I'm ready for something like that. And we've only just reconnected."

"How do you know unless you go for it? Listen, girl, you have firsthand experience of how short life is. You deserve this."

"Last night we ended up lying in each other's arms watching the stars. Then a kiss got out of hand."

"Shut up," Dottie said in surprise.

"You asked."

"I did, so tell me more."

"Nothing else to say. Jarrod's being sweet. He would have liked to take things further, but I'm not ready, and he respected that."

"I should think he would. However, it seems to me that you like him."

"I do."

"Your ex-husband sounds like a first-class a-hole, and he deserves everything he has coming. I can't imagine any father doing what he did or thinking they could get away with it just because their family has money. Well then. It's time to move on now, Maisy. Time to give yourself a break."

"Do you think so?"

"Yes."

"I know you're right."

"Focus on what's happening now, not later this month." Dottie took a sip of her coffee before speaking again. "I know it must be hard for you. How can you possibly move on? It was silly of me to say that." She took another sip. "But you do need to think about yourself. Your children wouldn't want you to be unhappy."

"Perhaps you're right."

"I'll tell you what, bring him to babysitting duties on Saturday, and I'll let you know if he's suitable or not."

"What are you, my mother?" Maisy laughed at her friend's amused expression.

The two women giggled, and Maisy felt better than she had in a long time.

****

Jarrod worked meticulously and speedily at pulling up the old wood and dumping it into the back of his Tahoe. It would be recycled and used for something else. His company used environment-friendly products wherever possible.

Maisy was never very far from his thoughts. The truth was he couldn't keep from thinking about last night. Her eyes glistened with desire in the moonlight, and her short hair ruffled. He had felt her hard nipples through the material of his shirt. She was aroused, but so was he, fuck, all he had wanted to do was kiss her until they were oblivious to anything around them.

His secretary had briefed him this morning of the day's schedule. Sheena had been with him since he first realized he would need some help with the administration. She kept him organized with minimal fuss; her husband worked as his foreman and had also been with him from the start. Jarrod would like to think he'd had a hand in their subsequent marriage.

Sheena took great delight in trying to find a woman

for him, and every time he went to their house for dinner, he knew there would be a blind date waiting. In fact, it had been happening for so long that he'd be disappointed if she didn't do it.

Jarrod decided very early on that work wouldn't rule his life, but he loved what he did. As far as he was concerned, it wasn't a chore. It had been an easy process to go on to make beautiful kitchens: original, unique, and reasonably priced. His two best friends from the children's homes had helped him in the beginning, hauling around trucks of pine and contributing to putting his designs together.

Even now, they still gravitated toward each other at least once a month. All three men lived in the same area of Washington, DC. Each had done well, considering where they came from and the unloved environment in which they'd spent the latter part of their younger years. Liam was a criminal attorney, sharing his practice with two others, and Max worked as an aerospace engineer and traveled the world, giving his expertise where needed.

Jarrod was more than a little worried about lying to Maisy. Why the hell hadn't he told her about owning the business? Why had he made it such a big secret? He guessed he wanted them to be those two carefree teenagers again. He was such a dumbass and a coward. But now he was afraid telling her would make him look like her ex, a liar. As Jarrod struggled with his lies, his cell phone rang. Max's number flashed up, and Jarrod clicked the button to answer it.

"Get your ass back here. We're heading to the mountains for some climbing."

Jarrod knew what that meant. Max had a cabin high

up on Beech Mountain, North Carolina. It was a small town with just slightly over three hundred residents, and it was the ideal spot for a cabin retreat. The three men often spent weekends there, climbing in the summer and skiing in the winter.

"Hey, dude, how's it going?"

"All the better for hearing your sexy, dulcet tones."

"Fuck off," Jarrod said as Max tried to wind him up—which was pretty standard, they ribbed each other all the time.

"Figured you'd say that. So, how about a mountain weekend?"

"No can do this weekend. I have too much work," Jarrod said, pursing his lips at the blatant lie.

"Shit, Jarrod, you're the boss—delegate."

"Special job, so it's all hands on deck."

"Jesus, man! You run a billion-dollar company and can't take some time off?"

He could hear the exasperation in Max's voice. "Usually, I wouldn't need to be on-site, but the customer is a friend." That wasn't a lie, but somehow it didn't sit well with him. However, he didn't want them to know about Maisy—not yet, anyway. "Why don't you and Liam go, and if I get the chance to catch up with you, I will. And if not, I'll come next time."

"Yeah, I think we will. It's been a while since we headed up there, and I need to blow off some steam," Max said.

"Problems?" Jarrod asked.

"No, just a big job that seemed to have had one problem after another."

"Tough one."

"Yeah, thank God it's finished."

"A weekend up the mountain sounds like just what you need."

"Exactly. So, how's your love life?" Max asked.

"Nonexistent," Jarrod said.

"Umm, that's strange. When I asked Sheena where you were, she said the job you're doing is at Nags Head, and it's for a woman."

"It is." Damn! He'd have to have words with his secretary, although knowing Sheena, she'd done it on purpose.

"Is she single?"

"Bastard. You knew all along where I was." Jarrod laughed.

"Yeah, I knew. Have to keep you on your toes."

"So, there is no weekend in the mountains?"

"No, I just thought it would be fun to torment you."

"Fuck you, Max."

"Not on your life. I prefer my companions to be of the female variety."

"Don't be facetious," Jarrod said.

Max chuckled. "So, who is she?"

"No one. She's a customer and an old friend."

"You knew her before?"

"Kinda." And he went on to tell Max the story of how they met.

"Sounds like something more to me."

"I honestly don't know, bud. I'm taking it slow."

"Okay, we have to make a date for the mountains."

"Yeah, we will."

"Right, gotta go. Don't do anything I wouldn't."

"Not much chance of that." He chuckled. "You're the man with a woman on each arm."

They ribbed each other for a few more moments

before hanging up. No doubt Max would immediately call Liam to inform him of the situation. Jarrod shook his head at the thought.

Chapter 6

Maisy spent the rest of the day pottering around. Her conversations with Jarrod were sparse…her choice. Her mind had repeatedly gone over her morning conversation with Dottie. Was Maisy ready to get into a relationship? Was she being presumptuous in thinking this thing she had with Jarrod was anything other than sexual attraction?

The emotions inside her when she spent time with him were something she'd never felt before, even with her ex. The intensity of her desire for Jarrod was as near to passion as she'd ever experienced.

A paradisiacal thrill traveled deep into her belly when she thought about Jarrod's lips on hers and the softness of his touch as his mouth moved down her neck. Holy cow, she trembled all the way down to her toes.

Jarrod had left over an hour ago. The kitchen and living room flooring had been removed, ready for the new wood coming tomorrow. He had even removed all the old flooring in the back of his truck. The company he worked for recycled as much as they could, which she wholeheartedly approved of.

His invitation to go out to eat tonight had surprised her a little, and her first instinct had been to refuse. But then she'd thought about her chat with her friend this morning and decided why not. They got on well together, and she hated eating on her own.

Maisy uncovered her canvas, intending to do some more painting, but she couldn't find the inspiration. The thought of finishing it unnerved her a little because when she did, it meant that was the end, and she wanted it to be perfect. She placed the sheet back over it and went for a walk instead.

That evening she spent a leisurely time getting ready. She wore a white shift dress with matching slip-on peep-toe shoes. The dress showed off her tanned skin, and as she surveyed herself in the full-length mirror she realized it had been a long time since she had dressed up to go out with a man.

Maisy waited for Jarrod to pick her up, and when the knock at the door came she opened it with a smile on her face, but that smile left very quickly when she saw who it was.

"Jack," she whispered as her whole body went cold at seeing him standing before her. She felt the pain as if it had happened yesterday. "What do you want?" she asked as she forced herself to stand up straight, although she just wanted to crumble to the floor. Every time she saw him the images of what happened that day came flooding back to her as if it was yesterday. "Didn't your bail conditions require that you stay in the UK and hand in your passport?"

He looked tired, older, and less tall than he had been. His raven-black hair had some graying patches that weren't there before.

She looked past him and saw a black limousine, a driver leaning against it with his arms crossed. Steve, the driver, he used all the time.

"Hello, Maisy. Aren't you going to invite me in?" Jack asked.

She looked at him, her mind blank.

Elsa sat up from her cushion and growled. She had never liked Jack. Maisy stroked the top of her head. "It's okay, baby."

This was the man who killed her children. The man who had been her husband—the man she hated with all her heart.

She stood to the side, allowing him to enter, then closed the door once he'd stepped into the kitchen. Maisy leaned back against the door. She felt physically sick looking at him.

"Don't look at me like that. I know how you feel, and it can't be any worse than my hate for myself."

His words surprised her—the Jack she knew never felt wrong about anything.

"Don't presume to think you have any idea what I feel. You have no right, no right at all. I shouldn't be surprised you've ignored your bail restrictions." Maisy couldn't help the bitterness she could hear in the tone of her voice.

"I deserve every bit of your resentment toward me. Jesus." He scrubbed his hand over his face. "I can hardly live each day with what happened. What makes it so much worse is how much you hate me." He seemed to stagger a little.

She reached for the only kitchen chair. "Here, sit," she said as she pushed it toward him.

"Thank you."

This was a side of Jack she'd never seen. But he was wrong if he thought coming there and showing her how much he hated himself would make her feel any differently.

"You're right," he said, looking at her. "I have

jumped my bail restrictions. Don't even ask how I did it." He stared at her silently for a moment, as if he were trying to find the right words. "I wanted to say sorry—a useless word—for what I did. But I needed you to know that whatever happens in court will never be as hard as the life sentence of pain I feel."

Damn. Why didn't she just kick him out? Seeing him, and listening to his words, just brought back the whole accident as if it happened yesterday.

"You don't get it, do you? It's not about how you feel, Jack. You have no idea how much I want to make you pay for what you did to Beth and Tom. Do you honestly think anything you say will make any difference?"

The pit of her stomach rolled, and she wasn't sure whether she could keep down the bitterness that threatened to come up. Swallowing back the unpleasantness in her throat, she clenched her hands together and closed her eyes for a second to try to get herself under control.

The sound of Jack sighing made her open her eyes. There was pain, deep pain, etched in those new facial lines. Damn him. She wanted to hate him. She wanted to tear him apart limb from limb. But how could she do that to Tom and Beth's dad? He may not have been much of a father, but they'd loved him. They had only saw the good in him, and not all the wrong Maisy had seen, and still saw.

"I'm so sorry, Maisy. So, so sorry. *This* is my life sentence, and I don't say that for pity," he said as he clutched his chest. "I deserve to pay for what I've done. But there is nothing anyone could bestow on me that's worse than the pain I have in my heart."

"What is it you want me to do, Jack? Forgive you?"

"Yes."

She was almost speechless. "How can you sit there and ask me that? How can you?" she said with a sob.

He stood up and took a step toward her.

"No, don't you dare think of coming any closer."

He stopped dead in his tracks.

"You think you can come here and tell me you're sorry for killing our children, and I'll forgive you?" She spoke quietly as the tremble in her voice vibrated in her throat, the pain in her heart never abating for one instant.

"Please," he said. "Please don't say it like that." His voice was low and emotional.

The rage rose inside her, so fierce that Maisy wanted to kill him. She launched herself at him. Hitting his chest, she thumped him hard, again and again. He did nothing to defend himself, just stood there. She couldn't help screaming at him, crying, and using both her fists to vent her anger at last. Somewhere in her mind, she could hear Elsa barking, but she could only focus on venting the anger she had stored inside her.

"Maisy, stop. Stop!"

She felt someone pull her away, and she struggled against the strong arms that were wrapped around her. She didn't want to stop.

"Hey, hey, baby girl, it's me."

She realized it was Jarrod and immediately turned into his arms and sobbed against his chest.

"I don't know who you are, but this has nothing to do with you," Maisy heard Jack say.

"If Maisy wants me to go, then I will," Jarrod said as he looked down at her.

"I don't want you to go."

Jarrod nodded and slipped his hand inside hers as she turned back to face her ex-husband.

Maisy breathed in deep and narrowed her eyes. "There is nothing you cannot say in front of Jarrod."

She wanted to club Jack over the head, but it would surely kill him if she did. She wasn't prepared to spend the rest of her life in prison for him. How he looked at her made her body shudder as memories of her time with him slithered through her.

"Well, hell, Maisy. That didn't take you long. You claim to be so brokenhearted, and yet you are already with another man, and your kids are barely cold in their graves."

She lifted her hand to her mouth and inhaled a sharp breath. "How dare you come here and tell me that the way I live is wrong…you…you *bastard*." This was the Jack she remembered.

"I think it's time you left," Jarrod said as he let go of Maisy's hand and stepped forward.

Jack took a step forward and squared his shoulders. Even like that, Jarrod towered over him.

"Who the fuck do you think you are? This is between my wife and me."

"Ex-wife," Jarrod said.

With a slow, mirthless laugh, Jack moved closer so the two men were toe-to-toe. "I told you this had nothing to do with you."

Jarrod drew Jack up by his shirt front with both his hands. "And I told you I think it's time you left. Or perhaps you would prefer if I made a phone call to the local police department?"

They stared at each other for a moment before Jarrod unceremoniously pushed him away. Maisy thought she saw hurt cross her once husband's face as he pulled down the material of his shirt. *Damn.* She started to feel sorry for him—and right there was her problem. She'd always been too forgiving, or soft, or whatever you wanted to call it.

"I know you find it hard to believe this, Maisy, but I'll never forgive myself for what I've done. Whether I go to prison or not, I'll be living a life sentence."

They stood to one side to let him pass, his head bowed, his body stooped, and she had to say something.

"Jack." She stepped forward, putting her hand on his arm, and he turned around. "I don't know if I can ever forgive you for what you did, but forever is a long time. You should never have gotten in that car knowing you'd been drinking. But you did, and with our babies."

Hot tears hid behind her eyes, and she gulped back the sorrow her eyes couldn't hide. The guilt was just as heavy on her shoulders because she should have known. She should have stopped him.

"But I was also to blame for not realizing your unfit condition."

"No," he said. "You were not to blame for me putting the key into the ignition and starting the engine. That was all me." He smiled sadly. "Goodbye, Maisy."

When the door closed, an overwhelming sadness ran through her as the misery finally broke her fragile shell. She collapsed into the chair and sobbed her heart out.

Jarrod went onto his knees and wrapped his arms around her. After a brief moment, he lifted her, turned around, and sat on the chair, holding her tightly until her sobs finally quietened.

"I'm sorry I involved you in that. We hardly know each other, so it was unfair of me."

"Do you think I would stand by and not help you if you needed me to?"

"No, I'm saying you didn't have much choice."

"I wanted to be here for you."

She leaned back. "I must look awful. I'm a very unattractive crier."

He lifted her chin. "To me, you always look beautiful."

Maisy stared at him. No one had ever looked at her with such adoration.

"Come on." She stood up. "Give me five minutes to tidy up. I think we were on our way out for dinner."

Elsa, who had been at her side the whole time, stood up from where she'd been sitting beside Jarrod's feet, ready to follow Maisy.

"We can cancel."

"No, let's start again. You wait by the truck as if you've just pulled up."

"Role play," he said with a wink.

"You bet." She winked back.

She went to the bathroom, and when she returned a few minutes later, Jarrod was leaning against the passenger side of his truck with his arms crossed. As he watched her walk toward him, he looked the epitome of sexiness—his sleek, muscled body apparent in black dress pants with a white shirt. Although he stood with nonchalance, his eyes narrowed as she got closer.

"What?" She lifted her eyebrow as she closed the distance between them.

"You look beautiful," he said as his eyes wandered over her in a slow appraisal.

"Is it too much?" She looked down at herself, biting her lip. When she glanced back up, she felt herself blush at his gaze. She'd tried to cover her tear-stained cheeks with makeup, but she knew she hadn't entirely been successful.

He reached out for her. "Absolutely not. I've missed you."

"Don't be silly; it's only been a short time since we last saw each other," she said as his hand cupped her cheek and automatically leaned into it. Her reserve crumbled. "I missed you too," she whispered because it was the truth.

Jarrod tugged her gently as his other hand settled on her waist. She could feel his warm body against hers, and she sighed as he bent his head and kissed her. His lips tasted of coffee, and his breath smelled of mint, and although her intention had been just to let him kiss her, she didn't pull away when he ran his tongue over her bottom lip.

Maisy couldn't help but enjoy his touch. "Mmm, this is nice," she said as she wrapped her arms around his neck.

She opened her mouth against his and encouraged him to take more. When he did, her resolve disappeared in a puff of lust. Nothing in this world compared to how she felt when he kissed her. It was apparent that staying neutral with him would be more challenging than she thought.

"Maisy," he said huskily as his lips rested on hers.

Her fingers slid through his hair, the need she felt rippling through her body like a giant ocean wave. "Hmmm?"

"I think we should go to dinner." His voice sounded low and gravelly.

"Yeah, you're right." She reluctantly drew her arms

away from his neck.

Jarrod's hands firmly gripped her hips, and she sucked in a breath at his look of hunger. For just a few seconds they gazed at each other, passion mirrored in their eyes, before he let her go, and turned to open the passenger door.

Maisy climbed in, and he brought the seatbelt across her body, his eyes never leaving hers as he did. She smiled before looking away.

"It smells of freshly cut wood in here." She breathed in the scent.

"It always does." He shut the door and walked around to the driver's side.

"I like it," she said as he climbed in. "There's something very fresh and clean about the fragrance of newly cut wood."

He looked at her for a few seconds before smiling. "Are you okay?" His tone was one of concern.

"Yes, I'm fine."

He nodded and started the engine, but before he put the vehicle into drive, he took her hand and set it on his thigh, covering it with his own.

They passed Jeannette's Pier. In 2003 hurricane Isabel had all but totaled it. Twenty-five million dollars was spent on the rebuild, and Maisy had walked along it many times since coming here. They pulled up outside Fish Heads Bar and Grill.

"I haven't eaten here before."

"Don't be put off by the name. It's very modern and has a good selection of seafood and beers."

"I'm looking forward to it," she said as he parked.

He got out of the truck and came around and opened her door. "If we sit outside, there'll be a fabulous view of the sun setting."

"Sounds lovely."

"Best spot in Nags Head to watch it." He helped her out.

Maisy felt his lips brush her ear, and goosebumps appeared on her arms. Her sensitivity to his touch shouldn't have been a surprise to her. Even at fifteen, she'd had such a quick reaction to him, but now that she was twice that age, they were more intense.

"Jarrod?"

"Yes."

She had to know if it was just her that could feel the powerful force that went through them. "Do you feel it?" Her breath stuck in her throat as she waited for him to answer.

"Feel what?"

"This. Us. Everything."

He ran his fingers down her arm, leaving a trail of sensations that made her eyes widen. He took her hand and kissed the knuckles, his lips feather-light.

"Yes, I feel it. I felt it fifteen years ago, and it's still there. Are we moving too fast for you?"

She stroked her fingers over his shaved jaw, kissed him on the lips, and then framed his face with her hands. "Let's just enjoy it and see where it takes us."

"For how long?"

"I don't know," she said truthfully. "But if that's not enough for you, I understand."

Jarrod kissed the doubt right off her lips. "Do you promise that if you have plans to leave and they don't involve me, you'll talk to me first?"

"I promise."

He smoothed her hair behind her ear. "Then that's

enough for me."

****

Jarrod sucked in a breath. Maisy was so utterly beautiful. Not just to look at, but her whole persona screamed good, kind, and someone he wanted to have more with than a short affair.

"I've never felt for anyone the way I feel for you," he said.

"Jarrod," she whispered, wrapping her arms around him as if she couldn't stop herself.

Her soft lips teased his, and he bent his head to accommodate, her tongue mating with his in a dance as old as time. His dinner reservation time had come and gone, but he didn't care if they were late. This woman in his arms meant more to him than being on time for food.

He ran his hands up her arms and over her shoulders, cupping her face. "You're beautiful. You know that, right?"

She smiled at him, and her eyes crinkled. "You're so sweet."

"I don't feel sweet, believe you me." He knew the hard-on behind his zipper proved that.

"I'm not all that hungry now," she whispered, her voice soft and warm.

Jeez, what kind of brute was he? He tried to think with his brain, not another part of his anatomy. "No, honey. Food first."

"Umm...I guess," she said as Jarrod untangled himself from her hold and took hold of Maisy's hand. "Thank you."

"For what?"

"For not rushing me and for knowing I would have hated myself for it afterward."

Jarrod lifted her hand to his chest. "Feel that?"

She nodded.

"That's what you do to me all the time, and I'm not going to ruin that by doing something I know you're not ready for yet." He raised her hand to his lips and kissed her fingers.

She smiled at him, and they walked into the restaurant. A waiter showed them to a table out on the veranda that faced the Atlantic.

"This is lovely, Jarrod."

"Isn't it?" It was already dark, but the outside lighting was subdued and romantic. "It's not the classiest place to eat, but the food is great, and the views are stunning."

He looked out toward the blue waters and was so pleased with what he saw. "Look, Maisy." He pointed toward the ocean. "Dolphins."

Maisy stood and went over to the railing, resting her hands on the top. "Oh my God. Look, they're playing."

He followed her over to watch them, and many more diners did the same. Jarrod made a sideways glance at Maisy. Her silky, soft hair ruffled in the slight breeze, and her smile brought warmth to her face and a sparkle to her eyes.

She turned and caught him looking at her. "What are you staring at?"

"You," he said, not even pretending otherwise.

She giggled. "Well, yes, I can see that, but why?"

"You look gorgeous tonight."

"Thank you." She smiled at him, and she looked relaxed and happy.

"Come on, let's go back to our table." He took her elbow and they walked back, then pulled her chair out.

"Thank you."

He handed her a menu. After a few minutes of silence, he asked, "Have you decided?"

"No, I can't. You've been here before, so you choose."

"How about fish tacos with sweet potato fries and a nice chardonnay?"

"Sounds delicious."

He ordered and knew she was watching him. When the waiter left, and she reached for her water glass and sipped the contents.

"So, tell me, Jarrod, what happened to you when I went home?"

He didn't speak for a moment as he reflected on his life all those years ago.

"You know I was in a children's home?"

She nodded. "I remember you were here with a couple of friends."

"Yes, Max and Liam," he replied.

"Are you still friends?"

"Yes." He told her about them and what they were doing now.

"What about you?" She looked at him, elbows on the table, her chin cupped in her hands.

"As I said before, I started to make wooden carvings to sell, and for a while, I did that, and then I became more confident with my designs."

"You are naturally talented."

He raised his eyebrows.

"I've seen the kitchen at your friend's house."

"Yes, it seems I have a feel for wood and a love of doing it."

"You're lucky to be doing something you love."

"I agree."

"You live in Washington, DC now?"

"Georgetown. I have an apartment overlooking the Potomac River."

"Sounds lovely."

They stopped talking as the waiter returned with the wine and poured it for them.

Jarrod lifted his glass toward hers. "To the future."

She clinked her glass against his and murmured the same. Her sparkling eyes looked as dark as the waters of the Atlantic Ocean as they stared back at him.

Jarrod didn't like talking about his past. The shame of what he had come from filled him with embarrassment. He'd built his company on the hardship he'd suffered, and it made him the man he was today.

However, he was mad at himself that an opportunity to tell Maisy about what he'd achieved had come and gone. Instead, Jarrod told her about his mother's death and how his father's disappearance had made his mom give up.

"I'm sorry, Jarrod. That must have been awful."

"Mom couldn't control her dependence on drugs."

"Oh my God, how horrid."

"It is what it is, but it was long ago, and I rarely think about it now. A learning curve, but I got through it."

"We each have a heinous past to bear it seems."

"No, honey. Your loss is far greater than mine. My parents do not deserve your sadness."

Maisy reached across and covered his hand with hers. He turned his over and clasped hers, bringing it up to his lips.

"Jarrod," she whispered, a little reflection breaking through the tone.

Before he could reply, a young waitress set their food before them. He reluctantly let go of her hand.

"This looks fabulous," she said as she placed her napkin across her lap.

"It is. Dig in and enjoy."

They both did just that, and an easy conversation flowed for the entire meal.

"Holy cow, I'm stuffed." She leaned back in her chair and patted her stomach.

"You enjoyed it?"

"Delicious. I applaud your choice."

It was the perfect evening. He would never tire of seeing her happy and content.

"Look at that!" she said.

He turned and looked at what had caught her eye. "It's spectacular," he said of the colors that were setting low on the horizon.

"The stars are like diamonds twinkling."

"Like last night," he said.

She blushed in the candlelight, and he chuckled. He was beginning to like the way she did that.

"You're gorgeous when you blush."

"And you are a tease, Jarrod Steel. I need to go freshen up." She got up and smiled before turning to go.

He stood up, watching her go. The waiter brought the bill. He gave him his card, and chatted while the transaction went through the handheld machine. Jarrod had felt like he was sitting with his soulmate today, and now he understood what that felt like.

Maisy looked in the mirror while washing her hands in the restroom. Her cheeks glowed with heat, her eyes were far brighter than normal, her lips entirely devoid of the lip gloss she had applied before she'd left her house.

She guessed that had happened when Jarrod thoroughly kissed her, before they entered the restaurant.

For some reason, she felt better than she had in a prolonged time and knew it was partly to do with Jarrod. But today, when Jack showed up at her doorstep, she had gotten a lot of things off her chest. Strangely, it almost seemed as if she had started to forgive herself.

Were things between Jarrod and her moving too fast? Was there a *them*? Did she even want that? Her thoughts whizzed around her mind as she thought about the last fourteen months. She'd come a long way from those dark days of the past. Maisy was finally coming to terms with what had happened, but it was hard to think of being happy, even now.

Maisy had never done anything in her life she hadn't planned until she decided to sell her home and relocate almost four thousand miles away. Now, Jarrod made her feel free and reckless but still secure in her skin. However, would she be able to curb her guilty feelings when she felt happy?

When you're a parent your whole life changes. Being responsible for that little human being is the most precious gift in the world, and she would always have those memories.

What guarantees did life have?

None. If she didn't know that by now, she never would. God, Maisy wished the impending court case would come so she could finally see justice done.

Absently, she reached into her purse for her lip gloss, slicked the pale pink liquid over her lips, and then studied her reflection in the mirror. She'd cut her hair short before the funeral. Now she fingered the short tresses, and realized that although she'd done it because she couldn't be bothered with the long time it took to take care of it, she liked it and thought it suited her small, round face. She was thinner than she used to be, and her cheekbones more prominent. The dark circles under her eyes were part of her grieving; still, sleepless nights plagued her.

Maisy had thought about whether she'd ever marry again. That had led to the thought of having more children. But the idea had been quickly swept from her mind. How could she? It would be like replacing her babies she'd lost.

She picked up her purse, turned, and made her way from the restroom.

Jarrod was leaning against the rails surrounding the deck where they had been eating. He turned as she approached him. He looked her over, searching her face. She smiled and stood beside him. They looked out at the moonlit ocean and breathed in the salty air.

"You okay?" he asked.

She nodded. "Yes, thank you."

"We ready to go now?"

"Yes, let's."

As Maisy moved toward the exit she felt his large hand enfold hers. Startled, she stopped and looked up at him. For a second she was memorized by the look of desire in his eyes. He squeezed her fingers gently, and she didn't hesitate in returning the squeeze.

They left the restaurant and walked the short distance to the truck, their silence comfortable. But as Jarrod shut her door and she lay her head back against the soft leather, she could feel her eyes closing.

****

Maisy heard the sound of tires squealing, metal

111

against metal, and screaming that she couldn't stop. She reached out to try and get hold of Beth, but she couldn't focus as the car turned over and over. Tom was shouting for her from the front seat. She tried to reach him but couldn't.

Each time the car rolled, she could see Beth with blood on her forehead and her eyes glazed. That look! And then silence. Why were the kids so quiet?

She tried to undo her seatbelt to reach them, but it was stuck. She had the most excruciating pain down her leg. Oh God, she tugged and pulled, but the seatbelt wouldn't budge. The metal clip seemed stuck.

"Beth! Tom!" She screamed their names repeatedly.

"Maisy, Maisy, sweetheart! Wake up. You're having a nightmare."

Her breath came in pants as she opened her eyes. Just for a moment, her surroundings were unclear to her.

"Maisy?" Jarrod shook her gently. His eyes held a worried expression.

Her legs were curled up beneath her, and she must have slipped her shoes off. When Jarrod squeezed her shoulder, she flinched. As he unbuckled her seatbelt, he wrapped his arms around her. For a second, she resisted, then sank into his warmth.

"You were dreaming, honey." His lips brushed her temple.

It hadn't been a dream. It was the nightmare that had plagued her since the accident. But she hadn't had one recently.

She couldn't hold back her tears anymore. She sobbed against Jarrod, the material of his shirt soaking up the dampness.

Maisy recognized being picked up from the car, and

Jarrod twisted and reached for something on her seat. She realized it was her purse so that he could get her key. Through the haze of her sadness, she felt Jarrod opening the door, slamming it behind him.

He strode through the house to her bedroom. Sitting on the bed, he held her while she clung to him, the weeping eventually subsiding into tiny breaths. He rocked her like a small child, and Maisy felt safe to close her eyes.

Chapter 7

Jarrod felt Maisy's weight go heavy, and he glanced down at her and saw that she was sleeping. Standing up, he turned and settled Maisy on top of the duvet, covering her with the yellow throw from the bottom of the bed. It must have been the meeting with her ex that had brought back all the memories of the accident.

Jarrod noticed Elsa had come in and laid on a large cushion on the floor. He waited a moment to ensure Maisy stayed asleep, then bent down and kissed her forehead before exiting the room. He left the door ajar so he could hear her if she woke.

Reaching into his shirt pocket, Jarrod took his cell phone out and looked at the messages he'd received. A few from his office, but nothing that couldn't wait until tomorrow. He needed a drink, so he went to the kitchen, where he found a half-bottle of Shiraz. Taking a glass from the drainer, he poured some of the red wine into it.

Going back to the living room, he opened the front door, stepped outside onto the porch, and leaned on the railings, making a mental note to replace its rickety wood. The night air had chilled from earlier on, the darkness only broken by the full moon.

Jarrod recollected the past hour. When he'd realized Maisy was having a nightmare, the desolate moaning coming from her made him understand the enormity of the hurt she still felt.

He told himself Maisy still had a long way to go. The open case would be a constant reminder of what had happened, and mentally her wounds would never heal until she had closure.

Drinking the last of the wine, Jarrod turned around and headed back into the house, locking the door behind him. Deciding to stay the night, he looked around the room and realized there was nowhere to sleep. He had moved the furniture out onto the porch earlier, readying the room for him to lay the flooring, and he didn't want to wake Maisy by moving it back inside.

Returning to the bedroom, Jarrod pushed the door open and stood there momentarily. Maisy was still fast asleep. Elsa had moved from her cushion, and lay at the bottom of the bed, only opening her eyes briefly, then seemingly happy he wasn't an intruder, fell back to sleep.

Maisy looked so serene, her chest rising and falling, her breathing calmer than it had been. His chest tightened as he finally moved into the room. He looked at the chair in the corner and pursed his lips. There was no way he'd fit in that. He'd have to lie on the bed.

Sitting on the edge of the mattress, he slipped his shoes off and settled on the other side of Maisy. He wrapped his arm around her waist and pulled her back against him. She didn't stir. He felt terrible because he couldn't control his erection which fitted very nicely in the cushion of her narrow hips.

"Goodnight, baby girl," he whispered and immediately felt his eyelids close. It had been a long ass day.

****

Jarrod woke with a start. Something lay on his feet,

115

and it was damn heavy. Lifting his head slightly, he wasn't surprised to see Elsa had moved more on his side than Maisy's.

He settled back down. The pillow smelled of coconuts, the same scent Maisy wore. She turned his head toward her, and half-opened eyes stared back at him.

"What time is it?" She stretched her legs out from the fetal position.

He checked his watch. "Four-forty-five."

"How did I get home?"

"I brought you."

"Yes, I know that, but how did I get to bed?"

"You were so distraught after your nightmare you fell asleep in my arms, so I tucked you in."

"I'm sorry you saw that. It hasn't happened in a while. I think yesterday's events made it all come rushing back."

Maisy's short hair was ruffled, but it was gorgeous to him. Jarrod smoothed his fingertips down the side of her face, leaned in, and kissed her forehead.. "You were upset."

She rested her hand over his and closed her eyes as he caressed her skin with his thumb.

Jarrod placed his arm on the curve of her waist and pulled her closer to him so her cheek could rest on his chest. "Want to talk about it?"

A long silence prevailed, and he thought she'd gone back to sleep, until her lashes lifted, and she spoke. "I don't remember much about the accident after it happened. But I remember the screams and trying to reach out, but not being able to get to them."

Jarrod put his fingers beneath her chin and tipped it

up toward him, so he could see the tears he knew were in her eyes. "Aw, Maisy. I'm so sorry for your pain." He leaned down and kissed away the salty drops of moisture from her eyes, the taste settling on his lips.

"Don't," she said. "You don't have to apologize." She reached over him to take a tissue from the box on the bedside table. "I think I'm doing all right, and then it hits me from nowhere like a tornado. It completely knocks me off my feet."

Jarrod held her tight against him. He didn't know what else to do, and to say he felt utterly useless was putting it mildly. "You don't have to tell me everything if it's going to upset you." His hand curved around the back of her neck, his thumb stroking her the soft skin of her ear.

"It's okay. You don't have to say that just because I'm crying, and you feel obliged to help."

"You want me to ignore how upset you are? What kind of person would be like that?"

"I think you are a lovely man, who has had foisted on him a grief-stricken woman, and you're too nice just to walk away."

"Let's get one thing straight. I want to know, and I want you to trust me enough to tell me…but only if you want to."

"I do. I do want you to know what happened."

He stayed quiet, wanting Maisy to tell him in her own words at a time that suited her.

"Sometimes when I sleep, their screams are in my head, just as if it was happening right at that moment. Then I awake, terrified, because I want to save them, and for a split second, I think I can."

"Oh God, Maisy."

"Tom and Beth were killed almost instantly. When their screams stopped...I don't remember what happened after that."

"Perhaps that's just as well."

She nodded. "I've learned to live with it." She gave him a pained look, and his stomach contracted.

"You're so brave, Maisy."

"No, I'm not," she said with an angry tone to her voice. "I completely fell apart. It took me a month before I could go into their rooms without breaking down."

Damn, but he felt utterly useless, and her sadness tore at his chest. How did a person survive such devastation?

****

Maisy liked the feeling of Jarrod so close to her. He felt warm and comforting. This big man lying next to her was so special she felt like she'd known him all her life. His scent invaded her senses, fresh and clean, and she squeezed closer to him, wrapping her arms around his body.

The thoughts that were never very far from her mind came flooding back as if the gate of a dam opened. It was like drowning with no way of being saved; sometimes she didn't even want to be saved, and the thought of not having to relive that part of her life became all too familiar. Her darkest days were when she didn't even want to breathe or live. However, Maisy had survived and had somehow come through the darkness to sit on the edges.

Her ex-husband had lived, and he did not deserve that privaledge. She should have felt bad about having thoughts like that, but she didn't. For her, the only finality would be to see justice done. Jack should have been charged with murder. When Jack got behind the wheel intoxicated he knew what he'd been doing! As a dad, it was his duty to ensure his children were safe.

But unfortunately, money had played a significant part, that and the well-connected family. He might as well have taken a gun to their heads; it would have been no different, but his family continued to spend money on the very best solicitors.

"Hey."

A finger tapped her nose, and she lifted her chin to meet concern in the eyes staring back at her. She smiled at him. "Hey yourself."

"What were they like?"

"Beth and Tom?"

He nodded, and she allowed herself the pleasure of remembering all the precious details about them.

"Tom thought he was in charge, but in fact Beth totally took charge. She always believed the best of everyone, and she trusted simplicity." There was an ache in the pit of her stomach that had never fully gone. "A definite planner, for sure. Tom used to call his little sister a bossy boots, and he was exactly right." She laughed. "Even at six, she kept a diary and wrote about everything." Maisy thought about those notebooks she still kept in her bedside drawer with the other writings of her daughter she just hadn't been able to pack away.

"She sounds adorable."

"Everyone loved Beth."

"What about Tom?"

"He loved football, what Americans call soccer, and played on the school team. Even at the tender age of eight, the coach said he had potential. There was nothing he didn't know about the game."

Jarrod offered her comfort by tucking her hair behind her ears with a tender touch she gratefully accepted.

"Beth drove her brother mad with the need to write everything down. She would badger him to distraction so she could take notes on what he had been doing with his day. She wouldn't give up until he sat down and gave in to her pestering. Tom's patience with her never failed to make me smile. He was a loving, kind son who wasn't afraid to show his feelings." The carefree way he would come for a hug…she could almost feel his arms around her now. She swallowed. *Damn!*

"I noticed the picture of them on your nightstand. You're children both look like you."

"They both had Jack's stubborn chin," she said almost absently. "I was in a wheelchair when they were buried. I shouldn't have been out of the hospital. It took six hours of surgery to fix my leg."

"Thank you for telling me about them."

Maisy tilted her head. "Thank you for listening." Another thought crossed her mind.

"What's wrong?" he asked.

"Jack's parents organized the funeral and paid for it."

"Perhaps it was their way of coming to terms with what their son had done?"

"They came to see me in the hospital, so I could help choose the coffins and inscriptions for the plaques."

"That's good, isn't it?"

"It was a rare glimpse of a side of them I had never seen before."

"Do you think they had an ulterior motive?" he asked.

"Partly they did. But, they were good grandparents, just blindsided by their very spoilt son."

"What do you mean?"

"They asked me to stand up for their Jack."

"What did you say?"

"He killed their grandchildren because he was a selfish man. How could they possibly ask me to defend the man who took away such two precious gifts? Tom and Beth were my life. And besides, it was the police who brought the charges against him for drunk driving—he was almost twice over the limit. Apparently, he had been drinking all day."

"So why has the court case taken so long to settle? It's been fourteen months."

"It has, but his parents are very well connected, and they've done whatever they had to to keep him out of prison. When you have money, a price will always be accepted."

"Damn, it shouldn't be like that."

"No, it shouldn't," she agreed.

"So this is it—the final hearing."

"Yes, he will be sentenced in two weeks." The thought of seeing Jack again made her feel physically sick; she had to swallow the bitter taste at the back of her throat.

"They are protecting their son, although it all sounds heartless," he said.

"Oh, they will do anything to ensure he gets the least time in prison. I felt bad enough I couldn't organize everything for my children's funeral." She spoke with huge regret in her heart.

"You were severely injured. There was nothing you could do about it. Did you see Tom and Beth before they were buried?"

She nodded. That had been one of the most complex decisions of her life. Maisy had been unsure until the last minute, almost not going to see them. The aching in her chest almost crushed her as she thought about them and how angelic they had looked. Jarrod squeezed her arm, and she sighed and leaned her head against his chest. She felt safe.

"Yes. I could almost convince myself they were sleeping." The sadness clouded her memory for a moment, before she carried on. "Beth had her much loved teddy, Mr. Mistoffelees, cuddled up to her, named from the *Cats* musical she loved. Tom had his Liverpool scarf around his neck and his signed football from the team. We had to let the air out of it so it would fit beside him." Going to the chapel of rest had been a last-minute decision, and now Maisy was so glad she had.

"What a lovely memory. But it's one you can focus on rather than on the accident. I know you won't ever forget what happened. But hopefully, the nightmares will lessen as time goes on, and only the good times will come to mind, not the bad ones." His fingers were smoothing through her hair, which comforted her more than she could admit.

"How come you know the right words to say to make me feel better? You always did have a way with words, you old smoothie."

"Hey, less of the 'old' if you don't mind."

Maisy laughed, already feeling better from talking to him. It was beautiful that she felt so comfortable with him. Chatting about her children, and at the same time laughing and joking with him.

The thought that she might forget Tom and Beth one

day frightened her, but Jarrod was right. Little by little, the special memories were taking up more of her thoughts instead of the bad ones overshadowing everything.

"Where is Elsa?" she asked, suddenly realizing she had left the bottom of the bed.

"She must have gone into the living room," Jarrod said, looking in the same direction as if waiting for her to reappear. "Do you want me to go look for her?"

"No, Elsa isn't used to being squashed up at the bottom of the bed, so she's probably gone to find somewhere to stretch out."

Jarrod nodded as she tipped her head up to look at him when he spoke. "I'll start on the floors tomorrow, and by the time I've done that the wood will be ready for the kitchen cabinets."

"The wood?" she asked.

"Yes."

"You're making them yourself?"

"Uh-huh. They'll fit better and look nicer. We make most of the kitchen furniture ourselves."

"Wow, Jarrod, are you sure you have time?"

"Yeah, plenty." He smiled down at her. "I love working with wood and creating something new. Every kitchen is different, and therefore requires a design that will benefit you and reflect your surroundings."

Maisy lifted her hand to her forehead and closed her eyes. Teasingly, she feigned a dramatic swoon. "Oh, I can't take the excitement!"

Jarrod turned on his side. "That's all it takes to turn you on? Obviously, I've been going about it the wrong way."

"I have no idea what you're talking about," she

teased.

He lifted her chin, so his lips were hovering over hers. She breathed in unsteadily.

"I've been trying to seduce you from the first moment I saw you. Now I see that all I had to do was talk about wood and kitchen cabinets."

"Please, the excitement is too much," she said, laughing mischievously.

He cupped her face and kissed her hard on the mouth. It made her heartbeat thud.

"Is that what you want? To seduce me?" She put both hands on his chest as she stared into his eyes.

"No, that's not all I want. I like you, all of you, everything that makes you Maisy."

"I can't… I don't think I'm…"

"Honey, I understand, and I'm willing to wait as long as it takes. We can take as much time as you want." He kissed her again, this time slowly and gently.

"I can't make any promises, Jarrod. The court case is constantly on my mind, and I must focus on that."

"I don't want you to promise anything yet. I understand. Take as long as you like. But I warn you, I'm not about to let you go again." He rubbed his thumb along her lips. "I'll tell you what. Why don't you put your painting skills to practice? Go out later and choose some paint for the walls. You can paint while I build."

"I would like to do that. When I was expecting Tom, I painted his nursery to tell the story of how excited I was. I painted small, cute insects, Ladybirds, because they are small, delicate, and beautifully marked with color. Dragonflies symbolize a change in self-realization, mental and emotional. They're creatures of the wind—their delicate wings move in the slightest breeze. And to have such a precious thing inside me sharing every breath I took, connecting in an indescribable. My life changed when I knew that a child would soon be in my life." She glanced at him. "You have this knack of making me say things I've never told anyone."

Jack hated the room and said it would make Tom become too soft. But her son had loved the little animals and had inherited her artistic nature. Throughout the years, he added more and more animals, from dinosaurs to cats, and even painted a picture of Elsa. It had been one of the hardest things to leave behind when she sold the house.

"I like to listen to you talk about your family, and don't ever think I wouldn't want to hear anything that you think is important."

Maisy's heart jerked, and she placed her hands on either side of his jaw, feeling the rough growth against her palms. It was the most natural thing in the world as she drew his head toward hers and kissed his lips. Before long, the gentle kisses had turned more passionate, and he worked her mouth. The earth-shattering kisses left her lips swollen, and she trembled in his arms.

Shocked at the intensity, she pushed him away before rolling onto her back and then off the bed. She went over to the window facing the ocean. Opening it, she wrapped her arms around her body and breathed in the warm, salty air. Even in the first light, she could tell it would be a sunny day. The sound of the water breaking against the sand was oddly comforting, and she closed her eyes.

Maisy felt Jarrod behind her, and when he slipped his arms around her, she couldn't help but lean back against him. His hands covered hers, and confusion fluttered in her stomach. She didn't know what to do with the sensations engulfing her. She felt guilty for the happiness she knew Jarrod would bring her.

He kissed the top of her head, and it seemed to Maisy that she was in the most special place in the world. Could life get much better than this? Did she ever think she would ever find happiness again in a million years? Was it even right for her to feel such pleasure in this man's arms?

****

Jarrod felt her trembling, although he wasn't sure if it was her, him, or a combination of them. He felt her breathing quicken, and he needed to be close to her. He couldn't help putting his lips to the side of her neck, feeling her soft, warm skin, and nibbling at her cute earlobe with his teeth.

Maisy responded to his touch by leaning her head to one side, giving him better access to her silky skin. Jarrod breathed deeply, letting her scent work over him in a veil of delicious sensations. Suddenly, without giving him a chance to see what was coming, Maisy turned around, hooked her arms around his neck, and lifted her legs to wrap around his hips.

He settled his hands on her ass, so she was coiled around him like a snake. "I wasn't expecting that," he said. "Great maneuver." He turned them around and leaned her back against the wall. "It's always the quiet ones you have to watch."

"You liked that?" she asked.

He captured her mouth in a hot kiss he seriously expected her lips to set him on fire. "Uh-huh," he said, as his tongue mated with hers—teasing, licking, sucking.

The urge to squeeze her ass was overwhelming. It was so soft, and fitted into his hands like the perfection it was. He hadn't expected things to get so out of control so quickly. The pressure of her yielding hips were almost too much to bear.

"Jarrod," she gasped, her arms tightening around him, her fingers grasping at his hair.

Fuck! He wanted her, needed her. Hardened nipples pressed against his chest through his shirt. His erection pushed against her, and it was impossible to stop the groan that came from him.

"Baby, you feel so good." He wanted nothing more than to feel her pretty flesh beneath him.

"I need you," she said as her lips covered his ear lobe.

He turned them around and scrambled for the bed.

"Shit," he said as they landed on the duvet together. "Very sophisticated."

They both laughed.

"And you started so well." Maisy's eyes teased him.

"Then it will end beautifully." Jarrod slowed things down. Leaning in, he kissed her lips. He wanted to be gentle with her. He almost self-combusted from the sexiness and promise she delivered through her lips.

"Promise, promises," she said as her tongue smoothed over her lips provocatively.

He started to undo the small buttons of her top when a little moan stopped him cold. He looked at Maisy, who was frowning.

"What was that?" she asked.

"I don't know."

Maisy disentangled herself. "Where's Elsa?"

She got up from the bed, and he followed her to the

living room. Jarrod's eyes trailed hers toward the kitchen where the dog was lying. Maisy was there like a shot, and he was behind her, crouching down. She stroked the top of Elsa's head, and Elsa looked up at her. It was obvious that something wasn't right with her.

"Elsa, what's wrong?" She settled her hand on the dog's head, and her fingers stroked her as Elsa let out another moan. "Jarrod." Maisy's voice was suffused with distress as her eyes filled with tears. She looked at him for some explanation, which he didn't have.

"I'll call a veterinarian." He entered the living room to get his cell phone out of his jacket pocket. It was early, but after googling, he found an emergency number. Jarrod stood in the doorway as he made the call.

The sheer panic on Maisy's face as she lay her head next to Elsa's was very apparent. He knew if anything happened to the dog, she would be distraught. Elsa was all she had left of a family that had been torn apart.

Jarrod spoke to the veterinarian and arranged to take Elsa to the clinic immediately. Switching off his phone, he slipped it into his trouser pocket before crouching next to Maisy. "We're taking her now. I'll carry her to my truck."

Maisy stepped out of the way, hovering behind him. He reached beneath the dog with both arms. Elsa's pain was significant enough to make the usually placid dog growl at him.

"It's okay, girl." Jarrod lifted her up and into his arms. "Grab my keys," he said as Maisy opened the door.

Racing ahead, she clicked the key fob and opened the back passenger door of his truck.

"Get in the car, sweetheart." But she just stood there looking at Elsa. "Maisy." His firm tone seemed to do the trick, and she climbed into the back seat and moved over. He very gently laid the dog on the seat so her head rested on Maisy's lap.

Jogging around the truck, he got into the driver's side, and turned to look at her. "Keys?"

"Oh my God, I don't know where they are." Her frantic tone was panicked.

They both looked around the cab, and he caught a glimpse of metal on the floor by her feet. Reaching down, he grabbed them and started the engine. "Don't worry. It's probably just something she's eaten."

Chapter 8

Maisy held Elsa's head on her lap. Stroking her soft fur, she tried desperately to keep the tears from falling down her cheeks. Big brown eyes looked up at her, the pain evident as Elsa gave out another moan. Maisy felt a hand grip her heart so tightly she could barely breathe.

She couldn't lose her; she just couldn't. Elsa was all Maisy had left of her past life—all she had that connected her to the children she'd lost. Her hands shook as she stroked the dog. Maisy lifted her hand to brush away the tears.

"How far is it?" she asked.

Jarrod put his hand over hers. "It's about fifteen minutes. I'll get there as quick as I can."

She nodded, knowing those minutes were going to feel like a lifetime. She appreciated Jarrod's deft driving skills. He drove as fast as he could, and because it was so early, there wasn't a lot of traffic.

"It's going to be okay, baby. Hang in there," she whispered, hoping she was right as she stroked the top of Elsa's head.

They pulled into the parking area outside the Outer Banks Veterinarian Hospital. Jarrod drove into a spot right outside the main door. Jumping out of the truck, he moved around the hood and opened the back door. The dog gave another yelp when Jarrod lifted her into his arms. Maisy got out and raced ahead, opening the reception area door, then followed Jarrod inside.

A woman stood behind the counter and looked up when they came in. "Elsa?"

Maisy nodded frantically; she could feel the hysteria welling up inside her.

"Through here," she spoke to Jarrod, carrying the now whining dog in his arms.

Maisy followed them into the exam room and stood beside Jarrod as he lay the dog carefully on the table. She winced as Elsa cried out in distress when the veterinarian put his hands on her stomach, palpating gently.

"Hey, baby, we're gonna sort you out." He spoke calmly to her as he took his stethoscope from around his neck and set it on the now rigid abdomen.

"Is she going to be okay?" Maisy asked. She was vaguely aware of Jarrod taking her hand and squeezing it, but couldn't acknowledge it. She had only one focus, and that was Elsa.

After putting his stethoscope back around his neck, the veterinarian smiled, stroking Elsa. Why was he smiling? Maisy couldn't tell. Elsa's pain quite obviously racked her body.

"Very soon, she's going to be fine."

Maisy frowned.

"Nothing serious then?" Jarrod asked.

"No, it's the most natural pain in the world. Little Elsa here is going to be a mom. However, I need to examine to see how far along she is. How long has she been like this?"

"What? Elsa...having pups...how?" She stammered out the words of disbelief. How was that even possible?

"Is Elsa in labor?" Maisy wasn't able to keep the incredulity from her voice.

She thought back to Elsa playing with the dog by the water, the dog she'd been friends with since their first walk on the beach. It couldn't be. She never left them alone...or had she? She felt Jarrod's arm go around her, and to be honest it seemed to be the only thing keeping her from dropping to the floor. Elsa let out a loud moan, and Maisy stood straighter, bracing herself for what was about to happen.

"I'd say she is about to give birth," the vet said with a slight smile.

Jarrod squeezed Maisy, and she looked up at him and frowned. "She was a little quiet last night if I think back, but we didn't hear her moaning until about an hour ago," she said, her mind searching for why she hadn't seen the signs. How could she not have known? Her stupidity astounded her when the factors were right in front of her—the extra weight Elsa had put on, how lazy she'd become.

"Okay, I think I need to examine her more thoroughly. Why don't you go sit in the waiting room? I'll call you back in momentarily."

Maisy stroked Elsa's head and bent down. "We won't be long, sweetie."

The dog was obviously in some pain. It broke Maisy's heart, and she couldn't stop the sob that surged up from her chest, escaping her lips.

"Come on, honey. Let the veterinarian do his job."

Jarrod guided her into the waiting area, where she sat down, her hands clasped in front of her.

"It will be fine, Maisy." He put his large hand over hers and squeezed them tight. She looked at him and smiled tentatively. She was worried sick.

Within minutes, the door opened, and the

veterinarian walked into the waiting room. She stood immediately to face him, aware of Jarrod standing at her side.

"It's my opinion we need to do a cesarean immediately. It feels like Elsa only has two babies in there, but one is particularly large and the wrong way around."

Her stomach surged with nausea, and she swallowed the bitter taste in her mouth.

"Are you okay with me doing it? She needs it ASAP," he said.

"Let him do it, baby," Jarrod said.

"Okay," Maisy said. "Do it, just take good care of her."

"I will look after her as if she were my own," he said reassuringly. "I'll need you to sign some paperwork while I get her prepped for surgery." He signaled to the woman behind the desk. "Jenny, can you sort out the release forms for this lady to sign, please?"

"Maisy," she said.

"Chris Doyle," he said, offering his hand to her.

Jarrod also took the outstretched hand that was offered and introduced himself.

"I've called in two of my technicians, and they'll be here any moment. Hopefully, we won't have to anesthetize her fully so she can be with her pups immediately. That helps with the bonding."

"She won't feel the pain?" Maisy asked anxiously.

"No, she won't feel a thing, I promise." He laid a hand on her arm and gave her a smile that eased her tension. "Should be about an hour. I assume you'll want to wait?"

Maisy nodded her head vigorously. She wasn't

moving from there until her baby was awake and okay.

****

Jarrod sat down and watched Maisy clasp and unclasp her hands as she paced the waiting area. Up and down she went, the same worried frown creasing her forehead. Elsa was so much more than just her pet. She represented the last memories of her children, and it broke his heart to watch her.

"Maisy, come and sit down. All that pacing isn't doing you any good."

Jarrod got up from his chair and blocked her path, resting his hands on her shoulders. She lifted her bowed head. The worry etched in her eyes.

"Sit," he said.

She shook his hands away and carried on pacing.

"No, you don't understand," she said.

"Maisy—"

"No, Jarrod, no. How can you possibly understand? Go home. I'll be fine."

He understood her words came from worry for Elsa. He sat back down and watched her continue the incessant patrolling. It seemed endless, and he could see that the more she walked, the more agitated and worried she became.

Jarrod felt helpless, and it was a feeling he didn't like one little bit. But he understood she was better left alone at this moment. He could only imagine what Maisy was going through. If she thought there would be a chance to lose Elsa, it would be the final stab of heartbreak.

Finally, Chris returned, and Maisy almost tripped over her own feet; she moved so fast. Jarrod took her arm to steady her.

"Well? She's okay, isn't she?"

"She is, and you now have two beautiful baby pups—one male and one female."

Tears streamed down her face, and when Jarrod put his arm around her and pulled her close, she leaned into him heavily.

"And you're sure Elsa is okay?" she asked again

"I'm sure," the vet replied.

"Can I see her?"

"Yes, you can, but she's still a little out of it. However, we managed not to put her out completely. She is going to be just fine. Follow me."

They followed Chris to another room where Elsa lay in a large cage with plenty of bedding and lighting, which Chris explained were heat lamps.

"Oh, Elsa." Maisy immediately went to her knees and leaned inside the cage, stroking her head. She opened her eyes and licked Maisy's face.

"Awe," she murmured and leaned her cheek against Elsa's face.

Jarrod smiled at the picture. It was the most natural thing he'd ever seen, and then his eye caught two tiny little bodies. The puppies were almost identical, eyes shut, and so damn cute.

Jarrod touched Maisy's shoulder, and she looked up at him as he crouched down. "Look," he said.

She followed the direction of his gaze, and he heard her gasp as her hand went to her chest. "Oh my God, look at them. Jarrod, they're adorable."

"They're a good weight and should soon be looking for their first feed," Chris said from behind them.

"Will Elsa be able to feed them, you know, with her stitches?" Maisy asked.

135

"Absolutely, and it's important that she does so they bond."

"They are beautiful," Elsa whispered.

The vet smiled at her, and Jarrod could see the relief in her eyes, which was very different from an hour ago.

"We have given her an Oxytocin injection, a hormone that will initiate bonding and help with her milk letdown."

"But…"

"But what?" Chris asked.

"The only dog Elsa could have possibly mated with was black and white, but the puppies have no black on them at all."

"Without boring you too much about different genes, it depends on what the prominent 'B' genes are as to what color a puppy will be. And a lot of science." He laughed.

"Oh, Jarrod, she's going to be okay," Maisy said as she looked at him.

She was happy again, and he so loved to see her smile. "Yes, honey, she's going to be fine." He breathed a sigh of relief.

"How long will you keep her in?" Maisy asked Chris.

"I'd like to keep her until tomorrow morning if you don't mind so that I can keep an eye on her. It will give you a chance to go puppy shopping. Since this totally caught you both off guard."

"You won't leave her alone?"

"No, we never leave our animals on their own, especially when they've had surgery and produced such unique little gifts for us."

"Can you give me a list of what I need to get?"

"Sure can," he said, moving to the shelves behind him. He gathered some leaflets and handed them to her.

"Thank you."

Maisy crouched back down, leaned forward, and gave Elsa a kiss. "I'll be back soon." She kissed her again. "Love you, my talented girl. You're a mum," she whispered.

When she stood Jarrod took her hand. As he saw her tears, he knew she was thinking about her experience at becoming a mom. He could see it in her eyes.

"Thank you, Chris," Maisy said, her voice grateful.

"My pleasure." He smiled. "I'm a sucker for happy endings."

A few minutes later they left the building. The sun shone, and the sky surrounded it in a piercing blue. Jarrod breathed in the fresh air, so glad everything was going to be okay. He didn't think Maisy would have survived losing her last connection to her children.

They got into his truck, and she leaned back onto the seat.

"You okay, babe?"

"I am now." And then the tears flowed.

Jarrod had been waiting for them. He took Maisy into his arms and sat there, letting the sobbing begin.

****

Maisy couldn't do this; she refused to let Jarrod see her fall apart like this. Pushing away from his arms, she drew in a breath and faced the windshield. She knew if she looked at him she wouldn't have a chance of keeping her self-control.

"Take me home, Jarrod."

"But, Maisy, I…"

"No, I'm fine. Please, just take me home."

Maisy could feel him looking at her, but she didn't stir from her position except to fasten her seatbelt when he started the engine. Out of the corner of her eyes, she saw him grip the steering wheel before he set off toward her house.

A short time later they pulled up outside her back entrance, and for a moment she sat, not knowing what to say. He didn't speak, and left the truck running.

Maisy unfastened her seatbelt, and at last turned to look at him. "Thank you, Jarrod, for staying with me. I would have completely panicked if you hadn't been there."

He frowned as he looked at her. "It wasn't a problem, Maisy, you know that."

"I'll see you soon," she said as she opened the door and got out.

Not looking back, she walked as quickly as her shaky legs would take her. She hung the key on the hook when she entered the kitchen and walked outside.

Inhaling the warm air and listening to the ocean, Maisy stepped onto the porch. Then the floodgates opened, and she fell to the floor, the tears flowing. The sobs she'd barely fought back now came fast and loud, and Maisy could hardly breathe between each piercing cry.

She was so relieved Elsa was going to be all right. She couldn't possibly absorb what it would be like to lose her. The thought made her cry even harder, and she put her head in her hands, releasing the worries of the last few hours.

The door behind her opened, and she didn't need to look around to know it was Jarrod.

"Maisy, honey, let me help you."

She lifted her head and tried to control the awful sound she made, wiping her face with both her hands.

"Come on there, baby girl. You don't have to do this alone."

His voice, soft and gentle when he spoke to her, made her cry all the more. The tears came in a flood of overwhelming relief she couldn't seem to control.

"Hey, I'm not going until you stop crying. I knew you were upset and sensed you didn't want me to see you like this, but it's okay, baby. I'm here for you whenever you want me to be, and I'm not going to leave you."

The hiccups were coming fast now. Maisy turned around and fell into Jarrod's waiting arms, giving in to the help she needed. He lifted her.

"Hang on to me," he whispered in her ear. "Hang on as tightly as you need to. I'm here."

Maisy encircled his neck with her arms and wrapped her legs around him. She breathed in the familiar scent that brought a comfort she couldn't explain and didn't try to. Jarrod turned them both around and went inside to her bedroom. Sitting in the big easy chair, he kept hold of her as he sat down.

"It was obvious you were scared and worried about Elsa. I know what that dog means to you, and how you've both been through a horrendous ordeal. You've relied on each other for comfort. So go on, cry as much as you want. I've got you, and I'm not letting go."

They sat for a while; she didn't know how long, but she felt consoled and protected, and it was lovely. Jarrod whispered soft words into her ear and stroked her hair until, eventually, her sobs lessened and her tears dried up. Maisy felt utterly exhausted and couldn't stop her eyelids from dropping.

"Hold on, honey," he told her again and stood up.

As her feet fell to the floor, he reached behind her and found a t-shirt under her pillow. As he helped her remove her clothes, she didn't put up any resistance. Maisy couldn't help the robotic actions as she put the sleeves of her t-shirt on without protest. She should have objected. He was undressing her. But she was way too weary of fighting anything or anyone.

"Do you need the bathroom, Maisy?" he asked as he bent his head slightly and looked at her face.

She nodded, and he led her to the door and waited for her outside. When she came out, Jarrod took her arm, led her to the bed, drew the bedclothes back, and guided her as he would a child. She did as he indicated because it seemed natural to do so, and quite honestly, she was exhausted.

Jarrod tucked her in. She lay back, her head sinking into the pillow, and watched as he toed off his shoes and lay down on top of the duvet.

"Come here, baby girl," he said.

Maisy didn't need to be told twice. She relaxed into the arms that enfolded her and closed her eyes.

"Sleep, Maisy. Forget about it for a while, and let me take care of you. I'm here. I've got you."

"Is Elsa going to be okay?" she asked, a tired sigh coming from her chest.

"Yes, baby, she's going to be fine."

"Her pups are so cute, aren't they?"

"They are."

"Jarrod?"

"Yes, honey?"

"How did I not know she was expecting?"

"I don't know how either of us missed that."

"I just thought she had a little weight gain, because at last she seemed to be settling down and putting the weight back on that she'd lost."

"Don't worry about it now. Go to sleep."

Maisy couldn't help but let out a sigh. How long had it been since she had felt so safe? It was a relief to have someone beside her. Someone, she could feel herself falling in love with, as she had all those years ago with the rebel teenager he'd been.

****

As soon as Jarrod heard her breathing quiet, he turned and looked at her face in the crook of his arm. His gaze wandered slowly over her features; her face so small and lovely, the gentle curve of her soft, pink lips, her cute little nose, and the long, dark eyelashes that now had settled closed.

He looked at his watch, and it was only just midday. They'd been up most of the night talking, kissing, and then the mad dash to the veterinarians. And yet...he wasn't tired. He mulled over the effect she had on him. Even when they were younger and barely knew each other, he'd always known she was special.

He looked at her again, smiling at the sight of her slightly parted mouth. God, he loved her mouth. Maisy smiled simply and kissed with a passion he hadn't expected. She was impossible not to like, impossible not to love... Damn, he knew she wasn't yet ready for a relationship. How long could he hold off telling her exactly how he felt about her?

And, of course there was the lie about what he had. He should tell her...he would tell her as soon as she had Elsa home.

Jarrod wanted to love her, and make her feel like

every woman should.

He wanted more. He wanted all the things he'd never had before with a woman.

It was impossible to erase her from inside his head and his heart. She behaved in a way that made him want to protect her.

Jarrod drew her in tighter, and she snuggled up close, letting her arm fall across his chest and her leg entangle with his. He silently groaned. Sleep was the last thing on his mind. But despite that, he felt his eyes closing with pure contentment.

****

Jarrod opened his eyes and stretched his body. Damn, he was stiff. He must have fallen asleep. He was immediately aware that someone was watching him, and out of the corner of his eye he caught movement and turned his head toward it. Maisy was propped up on one elbow, her short hair sticking up at angles, which made her look very cute.

"Hello, sleepyhead," she said with a grin.

She seemed much more relaxed. The sleep must have done her good.

"I need to go shopping for all the puppy things." She sounded excited.

He looked at his watch. It was just after four o'clock. "Yeah, okay. And perhaps we can get something to eat while we're out, seeing we've missed breakfast and lunch?"

She looked shocked for a moment. "You want to come with me?"

"Sure I do. That's if you want me to?"

"I do, I do, but I don't want to take up any more of your time, Jarrod. You must have work to do."

"Listen, honey, the only work I have now is your kitchen and living room, so yes, I have time."

"Great. I like your company." She smiled.

"I like yours too," he said as he turned on his side to face her. "Where will you put Elsa and the pups when we bring them back here?"

She frowned. "It's going to have to be in here, where it's quiet. There's no way they can go in the living room or kitchen, until you've finished working in there."

"Perhaps I could cordon off beneath the window, and you could put the bedding, etcetera, in there?"

She turned her head to look at where he was thinking, before facing him again and nodding her head. "There's plenty of room to set up something to make them comfortable."

"I have some bits of wood that would do, and it wouldn't take me long to knock out a little home for them."

"Thanks, Jarrod. You don't mind?"

"No, honey."

He reached across and ran the back of his hand down her cheek. Immediately, she covered it with her own and leaned into the caress. He wanted to love and kiss her from head to toe, lingering in places he could only imagine. He desperately wanted to show her how she deserved to be treasured.

Jarrod's pulse quickened with desire, but he didn't need an affair. He wanted their relationship to mean something. Forever seemed such a long time, and if someone had said that to him even a few weeks ago, he would have taken off at a speed where he would have been uncatchable.

He leaned towards her, and Jarrod gazed at her

beauty for a few seconds. It always took his breath away. He wanted to keep this vision of her in his mind forever, tucked away in the corner of his brain so he would never forget it. He couldn't stop himself from covering those luscious lips with his own. *Damn, she tastes good!*

****

Maisy shivered, not from the chill but from sheer excitement. Just a look from Jarrod had her heartbeat speeding faster than ever. She trembled in his arms when his lips pressed against hers, which incited a passion that happened every time he touched her. Her raw power of attraction for him thrilled her with an urgent need that took her breath away.

His hand slid down her arm and rested on her hip. He drew her closer so their bodies touched in all right places. His caressing fingers aroused a heat right through to her skin, which completely overwhelmed her. She could feel her control slipping away.

Quickly, his mouth became avid, leaving any breath she had caught in her throat. Without thought or explanation, she was utterly lost in the passion. With an instinct as old as the time her lips sought to give as much as she took.

Behind her tightly closed eyelids, she saw fireworks exploding, lights fracturing, and excitement mounted inside like a volcano waiting to erupt.

Beneath her palms, Maisy felt his chest's stiff, taut muscles. Her touch elicited a shudder of excitement from a man who was so incredibly gentle. She was far from frail, either in mind or body, but he made her weak at the knees.

Her breasts felt heavy, her nipples hard and sensitive against the material of her t-shirt. Already her mind had turned to mush. Jarrod's tongue touched hers; the kiss burst from gentle to hot and passionate, making her lose all sense of what was happening. Maisy didn't stop him when his hand edged its way underneath her top to touch her skin, and she felt tingling shocks down her spine. Strong hands curved over her ribs, his thumbs touching the underside of her breasts.

"My God," he murmured. "You're so gorgeous."

He leaned his forehead against hers, and they were both panting heavily. His thumbs rubbed her hard nipples beneath the lace of her bra. Never before had her breasts ached with so much need.

"I think," he said, "we need to get off this bed before something happens, which I know you're not ready for yet."

"How can you tell I'm not ready?" she asked. At this moment, she was bloody frustrated, and the passion inside her still fully encompassed her to the bone.

Jarrod leaned back slightly and looked into her eyes, and she blinked. His pupils were dark with desire. "Are you ready?" He raised his eyebrows.

Maisy gazed back at him, her heartbeat pounding at the thought of what he was asking. She didn't need him to tell her what those few words meant. The passion she saw in his eyes was fervent and unmistakably desirous, but he was right. She wasn't ready to put her happiness first…to let herself be happy.

He must have seen the indecision in her eyes because he removed his hand and drew the knuckles down her cheek.

"Come on," he said. "Let's go get ready to do some serious puppy shopping."

"Thank you for being so understanding."

"My pleasure." He kissed her hard on the mouth and sat up to get off the bed.

She followed suit, grimacing as she glanced at herself in the mirror on her dressing table. Maisy smoothed down the strands of hair sticking up, but they stood back up within seconds. Biting her lip, she hoped he didn't notice it too much. She turned to look at him; his mouth had an amusing twitch.

"Don't you dare laugh at my hair," Maisy said as she tried to smooth the sticky-up bits with her hand, only to feel them bouncing back up.

"I wouldn't dare, honey. You look deliciously sexy."

"Humph, Jarrod Steel, you have a very smooth tongue." And she blushed at the connotation of the words that had just come out of her mouth.

"I don't know if I dare reply to that."

"Well, contain yourself," she said. "I think it's time you left, before I embarrass myself more."

Jarrod hugged her, one of those firm, sexy, all-encompassing hugs that were so emotionally comforting. A sense of feeling safe and protected suddenly overwhelmed her, and the tears behind her eyelids threatened to fall, so she quickly blinked them away.

He leaned back. "About an hour, babe? Is that enough time for you to get yourself together?"

"Plenty of time, thanks." She smiled and closed her eyes for the kiss she saw coming. The softness of his lips gently glided across hers.

"Be back before you know it," Jarrod whispered against her mouth.

She nodded, and he turned to pick up his jacket before leaving. Maisy sat on the edge of the bed. It had been a traumatic few hours, and she breathed a sigh of relief that the worry about Elsa was over.

The two puppies were adorable, the spitting image of their mum. Tom and Beth would have loved them.

Damn, would this pain ever go? She put her hand to her heart and pressed hard, trying to relieve the discomfort in her chest. Maisy rose and stripped off her clothes as she went to the bathroom. She turned on the shower, and didn't even wait for the water to heat up, gasping at the cold before the stream started to turn warm.

The hot water felt magnificent, and she let her head drop so the water pounded on the back of her neck. Despite what had gone on in the last few years, and the pending court case with her ex-husband, she felt better than she had in a very long time.

The thought of those two little puppies waiting for her was precious, and excitement welled up inside her. Yes, Beth and Tom would have adored them.

Chapter 9

Maisy arrived at Jarrod's place a half hour later. She'd enjoyed the twenty-minute walk across the warm afternoon sand. Knocking on the half-open door, she popped her head in and called his name. She waited for a reply but heard none, and stepped inside the kitchen. Hesitating for a second, she could listen to a scraping sound she didn't recognize.

Going toward it, she approached an open door at the far side of the kitchen through the laundry room. There were about a dozen wooden stairs she followed down, taking her into a vast area. There in front of her, with his back turned to her, was Jarrod sanding down some wood.

"Hey," she said. "Someone is busy."

He turned around, and she immediately saw the pleasure in his eyes. Jarrod looked her up and down, making her tingle all over.

"Wasn't I supposed to pick you up?" he said.

"I know, but I was ready early and fancied a walk. What are you doing?" she asked stepping closer.

"Making Elsa and her pups a little place to stay."

She looked at him in surprise. "You've done this now?"

He nodded as his hand smoothed along the wood. "I already had the wood." He gestured to a part of the garage full of different kinds of timber.

"So what? You put this together in an hour or so?"

"Uh-huh," he said with a grin.

"Oh my God, Jarrod, it's amazing." It mirrored a child's playpen, with a corner designated for Elsa to feed her pups.

His lips formed a slightly bashful smile. "Thanks."

Maisy looked around what she now realized was his workshop. She noticed shelves full of carved animals, some small, some standing tall on the floor.

"Those are beautiful!" She pointed toward the delicately crafted woodwork. She walked over to them, trailing her fingers over the expertly smoothed lines. The intricate detail was out of this world.

"It's just something I do as a hobby."

"You could sell these. How long did it take you to do this one?" She pointed to the dolphin.

"About six weeks."

"Jarrod, you have a real talent. I'm impressed."

"Don't sound so surprised." He chuckled.

"How did you get into it?"

"I've been doing them since I was a teenager. I like wood…the feel, the smell."

"And now you make kitchens."

He nodded.

"You could make a fortune with these."

A funny expression crossed his face, which she couldn't make out, but it bothered her, and she didn't know why.

"You are truly gifted, Jarrod."

"I don't know about that. I just enjoy it."

Maisy stood for a moment and watched while he sanded what would be home for the puppies and Elsa.

"You know, I was thinking," he said to her as he continued working.

Maisy walked toward him and fingered the wood he was working on.

He stood back to admire the work he had just done and, seemingly satisfied, he put the sandpaper on his workbench and rubbed his hands together, brushing the sawdust from his hands.

"So…what were you thinking?" she asked, watching the dust particles fly into the air.

He looked at her as if he was trying to find the right words. "Your living room and kitchen are all torn up now."

"Yes?" she said, unsure of where this was going.

"It's not a very healthy environment for Elsa and her two babies."

She had been thinking the same thing but didn't know what else to do. "I agree, but there isn't much I can do about that."

"Move in here."

"What?" She widened her eyes.

"It makes sense," he said. "And then I can finish the work on your house without worrying about disturbing the little family."

"But I can't do that. This isn't your house, and your boss will get mad if you don't go back to work soon."

"I've taken vacation time, and I checked in with my friend who owns the beach house this morning, and they won't be back here for months."

Jarrod leaned against the bench and folded his arms across his broad chest. He looked so utterly sexy, from the top of his blond head to his large feet. Powerful, a man who was confident in himself. But there was something she couldn't put her finger on, something that seemed to be bothering him…but what, she couldn't tell.

"I don't know, Jarrod. It would be better for Elsa, but I'm not sure if it's a good idea."

He tilted his head. "Come here."

Maisy didn't think twice about the soft demand and walked to him in a few steps. She looked up at him, and he kept his arms folded. She could see the desire in his eyes as they darkened, sending a quiver inside her belly that made her catch her breath.

"How are Elsa and the pups?" he asked.

"They're doing well. I rang before I came out, and the assistant said it would be all right to visit later if I wanted. But I'm not sure because I don't want her getting excited to see me."

"Yes, well, I know how she feels 'cause the same thing happens to me every time I see you."

"Jarrod!" She felt the heat in her cheeks burn at the intensity of her reaction. "I'm not sure me moving in would be a good idea."

"Honey, I won't do anything you don't want me to do. You can feel safe with me, I promise. I would have thought you trusted me by now."

"I do."

"But?"

"Isn't it putting temptation into an already intense environment when we are together?"

"I won't deny I want you, but only on your terms. Making love with you will be…" He scrubbed a hand over his face. "…something special. I can't even say how much I crave you, but I'm willing to wait as long as needed. I'm content to hold and kiss you until you're ready."

"I know. I'm not sure I can be happy without feeling guilty, and I must deal with those feelings." She put her head down, and Jarrod lifted it with his fingers.

"You deserve to be happy, honey, and you will be. Beth and Tom will be in your heart forever, together with all your memories."

"Damn, Jarrod." Tears welled in her eyes.

He gave a low growl. "I want to touch you, but there's varnish and sawdust all over my hands."

"I don't mind," she said, leaning toward him.

He raised his hands, framed her face, and leaned his forehead against hers. Maisy felt his warm breath as she closed her eyes, the feel of his lips on her skin—her eyelids, the tip of her nose, each corner of her mouth. Then finally, the gentlest kiss on her lips, so full of promise, took her breath away.

"There is nothing I wouldn't do for you, Maisy," he said as he broke the kiss to gaze at her intently. "To see you smile, hear you laugh after all you've been through…that's all I need to see."

"Jarrod," she murmured.

"Hopefully, the court case will give you some peace, some finality to the pain you've been suffering. But *no one* will ever want you as much as I do."

Maisy sighed inwardly at those words. The look in his eyes was tender, but not for long. The desire she saw dilated his pupils, making them dark. All she could focus on was his mouth, and before she could take a breath, his lips covered hers in a kiss that swept her off her feet.

She had to cling to him to stop her legs from folding beneath her. Maisy's fingers found their way beneath his shirt to spread over his back. The contact of his warm skin against her hands was strangely erotic. His muscles tensed underneath her touch, and she couldn't help but dig her nails in. Maisy felt him tremble slightly, and she couldn't believe she made him feel like that. Her desire shocked her. His tongue stroking hers was the most exciting thing she had ever felt, and she was swept away in a passion bubble.

When his kiss gentled, it made the soles of her feet tingle, and she melted against him. He always knew what she wanted, how she felt, and where to touch and kiss her. Maisy's longing for him went from sizzling to downright naughty within a split second of him touching her.

Gasping, they parted. She trembled in his arms, and as Jarrod settled his lips on her neck, gliding across to nibble her ear. And when she tilted her head to one side, giving him better access to the sensitive spot she didn't even know she had, he obliged.

"Maisy," he whispered. "I want you so much." His gravelly voice vibrated against her lips as he brushed a kiss over the corners before concentrating on her jawline. "I want to love you."

He kissed her with such soul, such intensity that it took her breath away.

Hold on. Somewhere in the daze of her mind, the word 'love' registered. *Did he just say that?*

"You're so beautiful." His voice was hoarse. Jarrod gave her lower lip a hungry nibble as his hands slipped beneath her ass and lifted her.

She gripped his body with her legs, her ankles crossing against his back. It gave her the feeling of them being whole people, rather than two separate bodies clinging to each other as if their lives depended on it.

The thick bulge behind the zipper of his jeans throbbed against her, beautifully animalistic. The stroke of his tongue on hers as they tasted each other was exciting, the titillation thrilling her. His mouth opened, and he glided his lips over hers in a passionate branding that blew her mind, extinguishing every other kiss she had ever had.

"Maisy." His tone ravished her. The vital need of his kiss created a desire which made her nipples so rigid the rough feel of her t-shirt against them was almost painful.

She was desperate. Desperate to touch him everywhere.

Jarrod held her so tightly she couldn't remove her hands from the hard feel of his chest.

They were breathing as if they'd done a ten-mile run, and when their lips left each other's, Jarrod leaned his forehead against hers.

"What are we doing, Maisy? Where is this going?"

"I don't know," she whispered.

He smiled, and she noticed the desire in his eyes; his pupils dilated at his arousal.

"I'm sorry, Jarrod."

"What for?" He frowned.

"One minute, I'm telling you I'm not ready, and the next, I'm practically jumping into your pants."

"Hey, I understand." He smoothed her hair back from her brow. "You don't have to explain to me."

"My body reacts to yours, but in my mind, I feel as though I shouldn't be doing this, being happy, enjoying what we have. It just doesn't seem right. I feel as though I'm going to forget what happened, forget Tom and Beth, and I can't do that." She frowned. "Does that make any sense to you?"

"Yes, it makes sense. But you know they wouldn't want you to be unhappy. And how could you possibly forget them, Maisy? You will never do that."

"You are so understanding. How do you do that? How do you know just what to say at the right moment?"

He smiled. "Because I wanted you all those years ago, and now I'm determined not to let you go again." His eyes narrowed mischievously. "Why don't we just make out?" he suggested, wiggling his eyebrows.

She laughed. How could such a serious conversation turn into something that sounded so easy?

He leaned down and kissed each eye closed, and the touch sent electricity through her veins. He smoothed his lips over her heated cheeks, then down to her mouth—and she was ready for him. When they kissed, it was like a selection of fireworks...hot, but beautiful too. She loved the feel of his tongue rubbing hers. As it slid in past her lips she sucked on it, eliciting a groan deep inside his chest. Jarrod kissed like a lover, and he turned her on quicker than the switch of a light. And when he placed his hands on her bottom cheeks and lifted her, she didn't think twice about wrapping her legs around him again.

Maisy couldn't stop the movement of her hips against his, and as he inclined his head and teased her nipple with his teeth through the material of her shirt, she couldn't help the moan that left her mouth.

She felt him move his hand to a more sensitive area, a place that was screaming for his touch. She wanted to feel the pressure, and the need to encourage his thumb as it rubbed that little nub of nerves was overpowering in every way.

Holy cow! She felt as though she had tingly electric shocks. Maisy teetered on the brink of something electrifying. The feel of his hardness was sexy, and as if he knew she needed it, he rubbed against her, moving his hips to match hers.

A climax teetered on the brink of passion, the impossible pleasure setting her whole body on fire. "Baby, oh God, yes, yes." She breathed out the words she couldn't stop, the huskiness in her voice something she'd never heard from herself.

She leaned her head back, letting the moment's intensity overtake every thought she had. Her heart beat so fast she thought it would jump out of her chest. The fireworks behind her eyes slowly dissipated as her breathing eased up, and she lifted her head to stare straight into Jarrod's eyes.

"Oh my," she whispered.

****

Jarrod couldn't take his eyes off Maisy. Her mouth was slightly parted, her breath coming fast, and she was beautiful. He had to control his desire for her; he wanted to strip them both naked. But this was all about Maisy and letting her see that she could have this and didn't need to feel guilty about wanting pleasure for herself.

"Let it go, baby," he urged her as she continued to gyrate her hips against his hand that was settled at the very core of her desire. Jarrod didn't want it to stop. As he slipped his hand inside her shorts and panties, her delicious wetness saturated his fingers, and he couldn't halt the groan that came from his mouth. He wanted to strip her, be inside her wet heat, enjoying those clenching muscles.

"God, Maisy, you're beautiful; this is beautiful."

"Jarrod," she whispered, her breaths coming in staggered pants. "Stop, please…"

"Do you want me to stop?" he asked, stilling his hand.

"Yes."

He started to pull his hand away, but she pressed hard into his fingers, and he stilled again.

"No."

He searched her eyes, and what he saw took his breath away. Fucking hell, her need was so raw, and her pupils dilated even further when he started to move his fingers inside her. He wanted to strip her clothes off and take her right there on the bench, but somehow, he found the self-control not to.

"Please, Jarrod," she whispered, her voice strained.

"Baby, what do you want? I will give you anything."

"I want you," she said.

"Oh God," he groaned as he pushed in deeper until he could feel her inner muscles clenching. Each time he withdrew and entered, his fingers became saturated with her wetness.

His mouth caught her gasp as her lips parted, and she writhed against him. Her body went taut as she cried out his name when she came uncontrollably against his hand.

"Beautiful, baby. Just Goddamned beautiful."

"Bloody hell, Jarrod." She panted into his neck as he continued to massage her slowly; he didn't want to stop.

"Was it good?"

Maisy clung to him as he kissed her.

Fuck, he'd never been so turned on in his life.

There was a ringing somewhere in his confused mind, and it wouldn't stop. He came to a standstill, and they both looked at each other.

He leaned his forehead against hers and whispered, "It's your phone."

"It is?"

He nodded as he drew back, Maisy still clinging tightly to him. "Where is it?" he asked.

"Damn! It's in my purse." She plucked at the strap around her and opened her bag. Taking out the cell, she looked at him sheepishly. "Sorry." And she answered it.

Jarrod was happy to keep hold of her, and he didn't want to put her down. Not in the condition he currently struggled to control. The hardness of a particular part of his body still pressed against her.

He didn't register her words until he heard Elsa's name, and then he was all ears.

"What's wrong?" he asked as she hung up.

"It seems as though Elsa is pining, and the vet's office asked if I would mind dropping by to see if I can help settle her." She bit her bottom lip, and his heart melted.

"I suppose this means I should put you down?" He felt her legs loosen from around him.

"I guess you should," she said with regret. "Perhaps we could pick up on this later?" A slight flush colored her cheeks, and she smiled slightly.

"I would like that very much." He let her down, slowly, feeling every curve on her body as he did. He refrained from groaning out loud, but only just. He kissed her hard on her lips. "I'll hold you to that."

"I'm counting on it."

****

Jarrod held open the door for Maisy to enter the vet's office. The room was bursting at the seams with patients, all vying for attention from their owners. A little ginger kitten was curled up on the countertop. Jenny, the receptionist, absently petted its head while she spoke on the phone.

Maisy approached the desk with Jarrod at her side, and Jenny indicated with her hand that she would be with her shortly. Maisy smiled at her, then turned her attention to the fluffy ball in front of her. Instinctively, she reached out to pet the sleeping kitty, which didn't flinch, and Maisy laughed.

Jarrod leaned in and stroked the baby fur. Automatically, the kitty moved its head and purred, pressing into those strong fingers.

"It's gorgeous, isn't it?" she said over her shoulder at him.

"He certainly is," he said.

Maisy felt his warm breath on the back of her neck and goosebumps tickle her skin. She couldn't ignore how her heartbeat accelerated as he leaned closer to tickle the kitten's tummy. It rolled on its back for him.

"Hah, typical, she's the same when Chris touches her," Jenny said as she hung up the phone.

Maisy was slightly startled as her mind wandered into the warmth of Jarrod's touch. Of course, she was referring to the cat's response to his touch.

"She likes you," a smile crinkled at her mouth.

He chuckled behind her. "What can I say?" He spoke unashamedly, and she elbowed him teasingly.

"Another man who thinks he can charm anything and everything." Jenny laughed, but her eyes moved to the man behind them, and they were certainly not smiling.

"Is she bad-mouthing me again?" a teasing voice asked.

Maisy glanced behind her to see Chris, the veterinarian wearing a pair of dark blue scrubs. *Ahh*, she thought, and then she understood the sparks were for him. The tension in the air was palpable, and Maisy wondered what was going on between the two.

"Good to see you both again. Thanks for coming in," Chris said.

"No problem. How is Elsa?"

"Mom and babies are doing well, but Elsa seems to be a little tense. I think it's because she's missing you."

"I don't believe it was much of a hardship for Maisy to stop by," Jarrod said.

Chris smiled. "I kinda guessed that would be the case. Follow me." He turned and walked toward the back of the office.

There was a row of cages, one with a sweet-looking cat wearing a collar, looking sorry for itself. Chris stopped to reach into the cage and stroke the little tabby. His reward was the sound of a gentle purr before he moved on.

"Here we go. The new mom and her pups. Hey, Elsa, look who I've brought to see you." Chris unlatched the cage.

"Elsa," Maisy whispered as she crouched down on her knees, her hand automatically stroking the head of her beloved dog.

Elsa licked her face as Maisy leaned in to kiss the top of her head. It tickled, and she giggled a little, so happy to see her.

"Oh, baby, I'm happy to see you too. How're these gorgeous babies?"

The puppies were fast asleep, cuddled up like two little balls of fluff. Elsa had one paw around them to protect her little family; it was so charming.

"Can she come home tomorrow?" Maisy asked

Chris as she stood up. Jarrod took her place, petting Elsa and using his fingers to ruffle the baby fur on the pups.

"Yes, anytime after ten-thirty, when surgery is over for the morning."

"Great," she said.

"I gave you a list of things you'll need for the pups, right?"

"Yes. We're going to the mall to get the supplies as soon as we leave here."

"What about Elsa?" Jarrod stood up from where he had been petting the dog. "Does she need any special care?"

"Elsa will need some TLC. And supplementary feeding gives her more calories, which will allow her to produce more milk. Keep her food dish full all the time to begin with, so she can snack."

"Any particular food?" Maisy asked.

"I prefer to use a certain brand." He named one she had already used, so she was happy about that. "Make sure she's producing enough milk for both the pups and that there's no sign of infection."

Chris sat on the edge of his desk and folded his arms. It was clearly evident he loved animals from the way he stopped to pet the cat in the cage next to Elsa. But the look in his eyes when he talked about the care for her dog made Maisy absolutely certain that Elsa had received the very best care.

"Where's the best place for her to be when she comes home?" Jarrod asked, his fingers inadvertently squeezing her hip as if it was the most natural thing to do.

"Anywhere she's comfortable. She'll need lots of peace and quiet with no loud noises. It will be about eight weeks before she returns to her regular habits."

Jarrod nodded, and Maisy realized she would either have to stop the work on her house for eight weeks, which would be pretty hard seeing that the floors had already been taken up and the kitchen was half out, or she would have to take Jarrod up on his offer to move in with him until the renovations were completed. She frowned when she realized the thought didn't bother her that much at all.

"Thanks for your help, Chris. I do appreciate it," Maisy said.

"My pleasure. If you have any concerns or problems, contact me anytime. It was an unexpected delivery, but all's well that ends well, eh?"

That charming smile probably made many a girl's heart swoon. She wondered again what, if anything, was going on between Jenny and Chris.

Maisy scooted down to stroke Elsa, leaned down further to kiss the top of her head, and was rewarded with a big, sloppy lick. "It's okay, baby," she whispered. "I'll be back for you tomorrow."

She wiped a tear from her cheek before standing up, and Jarrod took her hand in his, squeezing her fingers gently.

"Are you okay?" He leaned down slightly and looked into her eyes.

Maisy looked up at him and smiled. "Yes, I'm fine."

There was something very heartwarming and precious when a man asked you that with such a look of care in his eyes. Everything about him muddled her senses. The more she tried to deny it, the more it refused to go away.

Her life after the accident had been about getting

past every second, then every minute, until eventually, she got through a whole day without breaking down. She thought she never deserved happiness again, not while her children weren't alive to share it with her.

Now she found herself thinking about having a life, being loved, and being in love. Could she allow herself to think her life could get better, that she deserved to have a little happiness without feeling guilty?

After losing Beth and Tom, she hadn't thought she'd ever smile again for an instant, nor did she want to. She squeezed the fingers that surrounded hers before letting them go to follow Chris out of the room. She felt Jarrod's eyes on her, sending a shiver of excitement up her spine. Yes, she was ready to move on. She just had to get through the trial, and finally, she could.

Chapter 10

Maisy loved shopping with Jarrod. He was so easy-going, funny, and kind. He chatted with the assistants, oblivious to their flirting, which made her smile. On the way back from the mall, they traveled in silence. She knew he understood she needed time to consider his offer for her to stay with him.

She knew he was right, and that Elsa and the puppies needed peace, but she didn't know if doing it would be safe for her heart. Yet it made perfect sense to move in with him until the renovations were done to her new home. However, she thought about the wisdom of spending her nights beneath his roof with that undeniable chemistry between them being so palpable, and she would be a fool if she tried to think otherwise. Jarrod was kind, gentle, passionate, honest, and these were all the traits she admired in a man.

Maisy hated making decisions. She didn't have a good track record with men; one only had to look at her ex-husband to see that. But one thing was sure—their attraction would always be there. She knew Jarrod would respect her wishes completely.

Was she ready to give herself that chance? Did it mean that finally, she would allow herself perhaps a little happiness? That feeling of guilt she had when she thought about being happy was awful.

"So," he said, "shall I unload the shopping here or

at my place?"

Maisy looked out the window, realizing the car had stopped at her house. She stared for a moment at her back door. Before turning her head, she looked into the eyes of the man beside her.

She was sure his eyes were never the same shade of green. Sometimes they were bright and teasing, then, when he was kissing her, and being passionate, they were almost emerald. But today, they resembled the sea, light green with flecks of blue.

The engine purred while Jarrod rested his hands on the steering wheel. His expression didn't give anything away. She wasn't sure whether this was a good idea or not. It made sense for her to say yes. However, would it be good for her emotionally? Was she strong enough to cope with whatever their friendship would become? The tenseness was already evident from the passion they shared for each other. Once the desire they shared was exhausted, would that be the end?

Damn, she had to just go with whatever the future held. She couldn't keep riding on the wave of emotions from the past. She had to let go if she was ever to have some existence, a life without her children. Take life by the horns and give it a bloody good yank.

"Let me run in and pick up a few essentials," she said.

He nodded. "Good. I have to come back tomorrow, the wood for the floors and kitchen will be delivered. So, if you want anything big, I'll pick it up then."

"You must sort out an invoice for me so I can reimburse you."

"Don't worry about that now."

Maisy did something she had never done before

with any man. She leaned toward him, cupped his face, and enjoyed the surprise in his eyes before she let her lips gently touch his. Jarrod didn't move, letting her decide just how far she wanted to go.

She stayed like that for a few precious moments, closing her eyes as she breathed in his scent, that faint smell of sawdust mixed with cedar and the amber of his cologne. Her lips moved slowly at first. When she felt him respond, that was it, she couldn't control the craving, the eagerness with which she wanted to feel his passion for her.

Jarrod drew her even closer, until only the middle console stopped her from sitting on his lap. Her head spun with his taste, and when he stroked his tongue against hers, it made her heart skip a beat. Desirous intent filled her body with a desperate need for him, the need to discover more of him than she already had.

It never ceased to amaze her how intense her feelings for Jarrod were. The kiss was explosive—it always was with him—and her mind blacked out everything but the here and now for a few seconds.

She swallowed the groan from him, and let the pleasure of the sound vibrate down her throat with the sexiness it deserved. She wanted to climb inside him; getting as close as she wanted was impossible.

They were both breathing hard by the time Jarrod drew apart from her. His eyes were darker than she had ever seen before. He observed her as if waiting for her to deny their undeniable chemistry.

All off a sudden it became clear to her. The past, the blame, the fear, the unknown future... She had to try and move on. The tragedy would always be in her mind for the rest of her life. But she could either stay the way she was, or try and allow herself some happiness.

"That was intense." She tried to sound nonchalant, but failed miserably. A seductress she would never be.

"Just a little," he replied as his eyes narrowed.

She cleared her throat and went to move away, but he stopped her by holding both her hands on his chest. Maisy looked at them, and honestly couldn't even remember putting them there.

She looked back at him, waiting for him to say something, and hoping he couldn't hear the thumping of her heart which sounded thunderous in her ears.

"We seem to have more than a little chemistry going on here," he said.

His thumb caressed the inside of her wrist. She could hardly think with the sensation that smoothed through her body from the intensity of his touch.

"We do." She spoke honestly—there was no point denying it.

"That's what I'm trying to say to you. It doesn't have to be more if you don't want it to be. We can take it as slowly as you like, and see where we end up."

"I'd like that. Thank you, Jarrod, for being so understanding."

"Just you and me, Maisy, one step at a time."

The craziest feeling she had was that she would have to keep a tight rein on her heart, because Maisy recognized it would be far too easy to fall in love with this man if she allowed herself that privilege.

****

They decided to go out for a walk after dinner. Jarrod took Maisy's hand as they stepped out the door and went down the wooden decking to the warm beach sand. The sky was cloudless, and the sun still warm despite it being early evening. She smiled up at him as she tightened her fingers around his.

The surfers took advantage of the high waves coming off the Atlantic Ocean and crashing onto the sand. The breeze ruffled Maisy's short hair, and Jarrod had an irresistible urge to push it back from her face and kiss her, but he denied himself that pleasure and walked in silence.

They'd walked as far as the pier; the sun was hidden from them as they stood beneath it. He stopped, and she turned around to face him.

She looked up at him in surprise as he put his hands on her hips and dipped down a little so they were face to face when she tried to avoid his gaze.

"What?" she asked him.

"Seriously, Maisy? You're so quiet. What's wrong?" He narrowed his eyes as he waited for her to answer.

"I didn't want to ruin this, us, the evening."

"And how could you possibly do that?"

"By tainting it with thoughts of the upcoming court case."

"I know it's going to be tough for you to go back and see Jack. It will remind me of all the heartache, but I can come with you and give you the support you need."

"Thank you. It means a lot that you would offer to come with me. But I need to do this on my own."

"We'll see." He wouldn't be letting her go on her own.

"You can't possibly take any more time off work. I don't want to be responsible for getting you fired."

Damn, that lie was going to bite him in the ass. He should say something now. Why was he keeping it a secret? Oh yeah, because he was a jackass.

"Don't you worry about me, baby."

She tilted her head to one side and frowned. "You must have a very patient boss."

"I have."

He pulled her close, pressed against her, and did what he'd wanted to do all day, and kissed her right there. Kissing Maisy was always full of surprises, like the way she returned his ardor full fold when he least expected it. The pleasure of knowing he could make her feel like that gave him a thrill all on its own. And hell yeah, he liked that.

Maisy's hands came up, cupping his cheeks, and he could feel the roughness of his five o'clock shadow scrape against the soft skin of her palms.

Her lips were warm beneath his. She opened her mouth up to him, and the feel of her tongue as it slid against his made him groan.

He could drown in her and he refused to wear a life jacket. The warmth from her touch was so complete, so meant-to-be, it almost took his breath away.

He slowly walked her backward, until she had to stop and lean against a wooden piling. He sandwiched her between it and his body, which left his hands free to caress her waist, his thumbs precariously close to her breasts. Loving the sound of her sexy little moans, he crushed his mouth against hers in a kiss that was a firestorm of passion.

He drew away slowly, wanting the taste of her lips to surround him forever. He cupped her jaw and used his thumb to smooth the skin on her cheek. They both gazed into each other's eyes. The pain she had suffered lingered, but he could also identify passion, something else he couldn't determine.

"Ah, Maisy," he murmured. "You are so beautiful and don't even realize it."

"I don't want to hurt you, Jarrod," she whispered.

"I'm a big boy, and I can handle anything that comes my way."

"I know you can, but will I live up to your expectations?"

"I have no expectations, none at all. It's you and me, and no one else."

She opened her mouth as if to say something, and he waited.

"This…" She lifted her hands to gesture all around them. "This is so beautiful. You are so patient with me that I'm not sure it's even real sometimes."

"It is real, honey. The kiss we shared is as sure as the passion we both feel. The connection was there all those years ago, we were both just too shy, and young, to pick up on it."

"Yeah, I guess. It's just… I feel so guilty sometimes, being happy. I don't want Tom and Beth to think I've forgotten them."

A tear slipped down her cheek, and he leaned in to kiss it away, the saltiness on his lips warm.

"They would never think that, but I understand why you would believe it. And I can't even begin to understand how hard it is for you to think about your happiness." He placed his fingers under her chin, and raised her head so she looked directly at him. "You have to decide whether to try and be happy, or to stay in a time loop that will only see life pass you by. Celebrate their memories by sharing them with the people you love, and don't feel guilty for moving on. Because, as I said before, they will always be where it counts—in your heart."

She nodded. "I guess."

"You'll never forget them, and there won't be a day when they're not in your thoughts." He smiled. "Let's just take one day at a time."

"I wish you'd known them."

"I do." He pressed a hand to her heart. "From here."

She reached up and kissed him softly on the lips. "You know you turn me inside out."

"Is that a good thing or bad?"

"I'm not sure. I'm still trying to decide."

"You do the same to me, so consider us even." He felt his heart give a little jump at the thought of her feeling the same way he did. "Come on, let's go back."

She nodded and put her hand into his outstretched one.

Just as they were about to step onto the decking leading to his house, he heard someone shouting Maisy's name, and they both turned around. A woman walked toward them, and the man behind her was carrying a small child. As they got closer, Jarrod's lips set in a grim line when he recognized him.

Mike Maynard had a string of hotels along the coast, and Jarrod's company had installed wood flooring and kitchens. Steel Homes had also built beds to specification for each room with wardrobes to match. It had been a tremendous job.

Shit. There was only one way this would go, and not in a good way.

Maisy greeted the woman warmly as they hugged.

"Well, look at you," she said to Maisy, standing back, but holding her hands. "You look fantastic."

"So do you, Dottie. How are you?"

"I'm really well, but hey, let's talk about you." She looked past Maisy to Jarrod, and although he didn't feel like it, he smiled at the woman.

"Jarrod, how are you?" Mike came forward with an outstretched hand while he held the child with his other arm. "What brings you to the beach?"

"Hey, Mike, I'm good." He shook the other man's hand. "Just a little break and doing some work for Maisy." He said it as flippantly as he could. "And who is this little guy?" he asked as the baby grabbed hold of his finger and laughed.

"This is my son, Sam. He takes after his mom more than me."

"Yeah, I can see that," he said teasingly.

"Darling, introduce me to this handsome man."

"This is Jarrod. His company helped with the hotels."

He looked at Maisy and saw the puzzled expression on her face as she frowned.

"Jarrod, this is my wife, Dottie." Mike had a smile on his face.

"Are you the man who did that amazing carpentry?" Dottie said as she held out her hand.

"Yes, there was a team of us," Jarrod said as he took her hand. "It's a pleasure to meet you."

"No, the pleasure is all mine," she said. "So, you and Maisy know each other?"

Somehow, Jarrod got the feeling she already knew they did.

Maisy stepped forward then. "Yes, Dottie, we do." Maisy gave her friend a glare that said *stop right there*.

"Come on, honey, let's leave these two to get on with their evening. Sam needs to be in bed," Mike said.

At that Dottie focused all her attention on the little boy who had fallen asleep in his dad's arms.

"Aww," Maisy said, "he's out for the count."

"He is." She turned back to Maisy. "Don't think this lets you off the hook." She pointed at her with a sneaky smile on her face.

"I wouldn't for one minute think otherwise." Maisy's narrowed eyes held a teasing glint.

"Umm," the other woman said. "Don't forget you're babysitting on Saturday. Bring your friend with you."

"I hadn't forgotten."

"Nice to see you again," Mike said.

"Likewise," Jarrod replied.

They stood for a moment and watched the little family walk on before Jarrod turned and saw Maisy looking at him.

"That's a coincidence, isn't it?" she said.

"I've known Mike for a while now. We've done a lot of work for him."

Why was he finding it so difficult to tell her the truth? The longer he left it, the harder it became. She would be so disappointed in him, which pulled at his gut.

They started walking back to the house, and Jarrod reached for her hand and slipped his fingers through hers. He could feel her hesitation. His heart raced, the thumping making him slightly breathless, but she returned the touch and he breathed a sigh of relief.

"Dottie is crazy, in a good way."

He laughed. "Just a little."

"We met on my first day here. I took Elsa for a walk, and she couldn't stop petting her, and somehow we clicked together like a jigsaw puzzle. She invited me in for coffee."

"She seems nice."

"She is," Maisy said. "In a short time, we've become good friends."

"That's nice." He squeezed her hand.

The night was dark, only broken by the stars and moon shining. The outside light clicked on as they approached the door, and just before he opened it, he looked down at her, to find her looking right back up at him with a frown.

"Are you okay?" he asked her.

She hesitated for a split second as if she was thinking about it. "Yes," she said. "Yes, I'm good."

****

Maisy's hand felt oddly cold when he let go to open the door. She followed him inside and looked at her watch. It was nearly nine.

"How about a nightcap?" Jarrod said. "It's still early…unless you're tired?"

"No, I'm not tired at all, and yes, a nightcap would be lovely."

"Come on then, let's sit in here." He went into the living room and turned on the lamps before preparing to light the log fire. "The night air's a little chilly," he explained.

Maisy sat on the large, corner sofa, the soft cushions making her want to curl up. She slipped off her tennis shoes and curled her feet beneath her, resting back. She appreciated the fire; the logs spluttered and spat as they took light and generated a lovely, cozy heat.

"What would you like to drink?"

She opened her eyes and Jarrod stood in front of her. "Whatever you have."

"How about some wine?"

"Sounds good to me," she replied.

He smiled, and oh what a killer smile he had. Jarrod went to the kitchen, and she heard the clinking of glasses. While he was gone Maisy took the opportunity to look around the room.

It was large, but still snug, and the fireplace covered nearly the whole wall. It was certainly the focal point, built with different shades of tan and yellow stone. The stone was beautifully abstract, giving the area a traditional sense, but without the bulk some fireplaces had when they were as large as this one.

The mantel elongated against the wall with a wooden clock in the center in light beach wood. Logs were piled up at either side of the fire in a slight recess built to accommodate them. The flames flickered. The heat warm and comforting, she couldn't help but stare at the hues of orange flickering around the wood.

The coffee table was made of a darker wood, and long enough to match the length of the very sociable sofa. Even the bookshelves were made of the same wood as the coffee table. The large bay window running from floor to ceiling to her right showed the moon peeking in, casting a glow of iridescence over the darkened sky mirrored by the Atlantic Ocean. There wasn't a breath of wind.

"Here we go," Jarrod said, sitting next to her on the sofa.

"Thank you." She took the glass of red as he put the half-full bottle on the table.

He turned to her. "Here's to…friendship," he said as he touched her glass with his.

"Friendship," she repeated before sipping the ruby red liquid and letting it smooth its way down her throat.

"Very enjoyable." She smiled at him.

"Glad you like it."

He had a gorgeous face, which didn't help her in trying to make conversation. His smile was so sexy, but warm at the same time. She'd never felt so comfortable in a man's company before. He had a way of making her feel utterly at ease.

"So, you renovated this property for your boss?"

He nodded, but his brow furrowed, which puzzled her a little, but she didn't let it worry her.

"It was hard work, but a pleasure to do, and I enjoyed every single part of it."

Maisy knew Jarrod had a great passion for what he did; anyway, she couldn't imagine he would do anything badly.

"You've done a fabulous job," she said. She hadn't seen the whole house, but she was confident it would have the same beautiful craftsmanship.

"Thanks," he said with a slightly sheepish grin. It made him look adorably sexy, and in the space of a heartbeat that desirous look in his eyes made the breath in her throat catch. Maisy took a large sip of wine to try and hide it.

He lifted an eyebrow, and his eyes were teasing, as if he knew what she was thinking. She stuck her tongue out at him, and he chuckled.

"What was that for?"

"Stop reading my mind."

"*Moi*?" His expression was teasingly pretentious.

"Ha!"

"You shouldn't have such expressive eyes." His tone turned from teasing to affectionate, and his arm reached around the back of the sofa behind her.

"Well. Then every time I look at you, I will close them." And she proved it by doing just that.

There was silence as seconds ticked by, and she wanted to open her eyes, but she couldn't. Maisy felt Jarrod move closer, and the anticipation of what might be coming had her heartbeat tripling.

He kissed first one eye, and then the other. She opened them and looked straight into his gaze of darkened pupils. Because she wasn't expecting him to stop kissing her, her eyes widened without thought, and she smiled tentatively. But the teasing corners of his mouth lifted.

Maisy's cheeks heated. She gulped at the wine, hoping to settle the roaming butterflies in her stomach. She smoothed her hand down her jeans, and her foolish heart skipped a beat when she looked back at him. Or two or three.

She couldn't help noticing the growing heat in his expression, and for a moment she was memorized by how defined his cheekbones were, and how the shape of his lips were soft but sensual all at the same time.

"We can collect your painting things tomorrow, before we go pick Elsa up from the vet's."

She nodded. "I'd like that, although I'm not sure when I'll have time to do any painting with two puppies to take care of."

"I'll help, and that will give you some free time."

"You're too good to me, Jarrod. Thank you."

His fingers caressed her shoulder. "I like helping you."

She was slightly distracted by his touch. It had been so long time since any man had made her feel as good as Jarrod did. No, strike that. No one had ever made her feel this good.

"Tell me about your marriage."

She took a breath. "There isn't much to tell. We met at a function to raise money for the school where I taught. Jack's parents were two of the governors, and because of their standing in the community, they were involved with the charity work."

Maisy remembered when Jack came to talk to her. As a new teacher to the school, and the area, she had no idea who he was. Besides, she always seemed to have her head in the clouds.

"Jack was a good-looking guy and had a charisma as smooth as a calm sea. But once you got past that it was obvious he had major issues. One was drinking, and the other was his uncontrollable temper."

She closed her eyes for a second before opening them and continuing.

"I thought I'd fallen in love, but later on I realized it had just been a farce. Too late then when we were married, and Tom was on his way. The only thing Jack had an interest in was drinking, and rubbing his parents the wrong way." Her ex-husband, she had learned later on, did not like to work, and had an eye for pretty women. "I didn't realize he had a problem with alcohol until after we married. Although I knew he liked to drink, I didn't know the full extent of it."

"You knew he had money?"

She nodded. "Yes, but I didn't know that Jack depended on his parents. When he took me to meet them, I realized he'd been lying to me all along. His parents lived in a mansion, and Jack still lived with them. Their home was beautiful, and I could clearly see how Jack liked the good life. The deceit with which Jack went about keeping me in the dark about his life shocked me. It wasn't about the money, or the fact Jack didn't work for it, but the knowledge that he'd lied to me."

"If you lived and worked in the same village, how on earth didn't you know?"

"I don't know." She shrugged. "It wasn't long before I recognized I'd made a mistake, but by then it was too late with Tom on his way. I thought his birth would make Jack grow up."

"But it didn't?"

She shook her head. "No, and to make matters worse, he became verbally abusive over time. One day I got fed up with it. Although I then had Tom, and Beth just six weeks old, I gathered us up, and went to stay with my parents for a short while."

His fingers tightened on her shoulder. "I'm sorry, honey."

"Don't be. It was the wake-up call I needed to get control of my life."

Jarrod drew her close to him, and she didn't think twice about leaning into the warmth of his body. He had the ability to make her feel good, and the conversation about her ex was soon forgotten as Jarrod took her glass from her and set it on the table near his.

Maisy returned his gaze. It felt as if he was trying to gauge her thoughts, but his aura sent a shiver down her spine. He surrounded her face with both his hands. She felt sure he would hear the loud thump of her heart as it pounded inside her chest.

Jarrod's lips came closer, and it was impossible not to stare at them longingly. They touched hers, and Maisy couldn't stop her eyelashes from fluttering, even while they were closed. The anticipation of the kiss didn't disappoint, and it rendered her into a topsy-turvy of excitement and passion.

In one quick moment, he pushed her back onto the sofa, and half lay over her as he continued to assault her mouth. Maisy felt him press hard into her, and how turned on he had become was more than obvious.

"Are you okay?" he asked as his lips wandered to her earlobe.

"Yes, I am," she whispered. "I've thought about this constantly, since that night beneath the stars."

"Making out like a couple of teenagers," he teased.

"Yes." She laughed. Maisy loved how he was able to bring humor into their intimacy.

He turned her so they faced each other as they lay on their sides.

"It will be even better when we make love," he murmured as he kissed her jaw.

"Uh-huh." Her breath stuck in her throat as his lips fluttered down the side of her neck, and she could feel the day's growth of beard rubbing on her skin.

He lifted his head. "This is going to lead to more than a necking session on my sofa," he said with a questioning look in his eyes.

She nodded. "I know."

"And you're okay with it? I can stop at any time."

"Yes, I'm sure. I don't want to wait anymore." And she didn't. She'd been putting off the inevitable, and Maisy wanted this, needed it. She had been kidding herself if she thought it wouldn't end up this way. So powerful was their connection, it felt like the most natural thing in the world.

When Jarrod got up and lifted her from the sofa, she smiled at him, and lay her head against his chest as he carried her. His heartbeat against her ear pounded like a train going at full speed, and she closed her eyes.

Maisy didn't feel guilty. She wanted to be happy, even for a short time. Jarrod was the man who without doubt would make her feel good. She had no idea how she'd feel afterward, but this was the here and now.

Chapter 11

Jarrod carried Maisy to the bedroom and set her on the edge of the bed. Kneeling on the carpeted floor between her legs, he smoothed his hands up, and down her jean-clad thighs. He reached around her and drew her as close as she could be in that position. No way would Maisy miss his very hard erection. The look in her eyes emanated desire, passion, in a look that told him she wanted this as much as he did.

"Jarrod," she whispered.

"Hmm?" He brushed her plump bottom lip with his, catching it between his teeth, and then licking it.

"I want you," she said against his mouth. The slight inflection in her voice made him swallow at how much her tone turned him on even more.

Jarrod closed his eyes and tried to calm himself down. He wanted to make it good for her, but the urge to take her there and then was almost too much to bear. He couldn't ever remember a time when he'd seen her look so inherently sexy. There was something very innocent about the way Maisy behaved with him. He allowed himself the pleasure of letting his lips wander down the skin of her neck, so soft and her fragrance so enticing it enveloped his senses until she permeated him inside and out.

Maisy let her head fall to one side, and he couldn't resist the little dip between her shoulder and neck. Her fingers curled around the covers on either side of her, and he gripped a little tighter, drawing her hips forward so she was right on the edge of the bed.

Jarrod couldn't help himself and scraped his teeth against the silkiness of her skin. The moan she emitted told him she liked it. He moved his hands around the curve of her waist, up past her ribs, until he felt the swell of her breasts through her top.

He took her mouth in a kiss. At first she responded tentatively. He let her lead the way, because he knew it had been a while since she'd been with anyone.

"Open up for me, Maisy."

And without hesitation she did, stroking his tongue with hers. He angled for a deeper, sexier kiss, and her arms reached around his neck, the feel of her nails scraping against his scalp sending a swirling vortex of heat straight to his stomach. Jarrod had always known she was a passionate woman, and he wondered if her ex had ever taken the time to give her the pleasure she deserved. He highly doubted it.

Jarrod's need for Maisy completely overwhelmed him in every sense. Perhaps she had been what was missing in his life? Joy rose in his heart with her; she was so easy, so natural with him.

His mouth wanted to explore every sumptuous curve of her body, but her lips were so addictive he didn't know if he could stop kissing her long enough to do it. Jarrod felt her tug at his t-shirt, and they parted, both breathing deeply, and he lifted his arms as she drew it off.

Maisy's eyes were full of wanton desire, and it almost undid him. He reached for the hem of her top, slowly pulled it over her head, and dropped it to the floor alongside his own.

His heartbeat thumped like a set of drums, and he was sure she would hear it. He focused on the dark blue lace of her bra through which he could see the hardened nub of her nipple. He couldn't stop himself from leaning forward and touching it with his tongue. Maisy gripped his upper arms tightly and moaned again as he switched breasts. As her nipples tightened to sharp peaks, he looked up while tasting the sweetness of the sweet flesh. Her eyes were closed, her lips slightly parted, and her cheeks flushed. God, her beauty excited him. When her lashes lifted, their gazes met.

In a voice that sounded gravelly to his own ears, he whispered, "Is this okay?"

She nodded. "Yes. Yes, it is. I want this. I'm sure at this moment, but I can't promise you a future, only the here and now."

It wasn't what he wanted to hear, but he understood. The court case would be weighing heavily on her mind, and she still had to come to terms with what had happened. If the here and now were all he would get, he'd settle for that.

Leaning into her, he kissed her. More than just a kiss; it was a promise to take things as slowly as she needed, at her pace. He was more than happy to do that. He savored her, made himself keep it measured as his lips discovered each and every curvature of her mouth.

"I love your bra. Do your panties match?" Jarrod whispered against her lips.

"I love nice lingerie," she said as her beautiful breasts heaved with her deep breathing. "Why don't you take off my jeans and find out?"

Maisy shocked him then by pushing him away—but only to stand up; he had to shuffle back slightly. Jarrod looked up and saw the invitation in her eyes. He looked down at the zipper facing him and had to draw in a very shaky breath. He teased his senses slowly as he undid the button and drew the zipper down. He saw the slip of material, which confirmed that her panties matched. *Fucking hell.*

With hands shaking, he pulled the jeans down over her legs, and she stepped out of them. As the heat uncurled in his abdomen, he let his gaze wander back up those slim legs to the part of her that made his heart race. He could see the blonde thatch through the lace that covered her womanhood, and fire ripped through him as he ran his fingers along the inside edge of the beautiful material.

Lust pounded behind the zipper of his own jeans, and he wasn't sure he'd be able to hold back for long. He noticed some scarring around her hip, but his gaze quickly went back to what predominantly he was invested in. Her back arched, she gave a soft moan, and he breathed in deep the scent of her, his lips just a whisper away from what hid behind the lace.

Jarrod stood up and searched her face. "Okay?"

She looked at him and nodded, her eyes dark and her lips moist. He couldn't help but take her mouth with his, and as his hands curved around her hips, he pulled her hard against him.

He was painfully hard. Oh God, so fucking hard. His lips settled on her neck, and taking the silky skin between his teeth, he gently scraped along the flesh while reaching behind her to unclip her bra, letting it fall to the floor.

Her glorious bosom was ripe and succulent. Jarrod's fingers drew across her collarbone and down between the valley of the plump skin. With the tip of his finger, he traced along the top of her bosom, then traced around the pebbled skin surrounding her nipple.

She was a goddess. Her breasts were perfect globes of sexy, pliant flesh. Desire ripped through him, a blinding light of primal hunger. Jarrod felt Maisy's fingers undoing the button of his jeans and the rasp of her knuckles on his hardness. It generated a power surge between them like he'd never known.

Jarrod could not imagine lasting long if she didn't stop what she was doing, so he stopped her by putting his hand over hers. He closed his eyes for a moment before taking her fingers up to his mouth and kissing them. Even that erotized his senses.

"Maisy, honey, stop."

He saw the hurt look in her eyes and knew she didn't understand.

"I'm so close, baby, and if you carry on doing what you were, I won't be able to control myself," he whispered hoarsely.

His hands curved around the flesh of her ass, and he lifted her. She immediately curled her legs around his hips, and a gasp escaped her lips as he tried to get them both onto the bed. Their breaths mingled in intimate confession, and before he could put her down gently, they both fell onto the covers.

Maisy laughed as he tried not to flatten her.

"Are you okay?" he asked.

"Oh yes, I'm more than okay." She lifted her hips, staring into his eyes with a glazed expression.

Jarrod pressed hard into her, and a low rumble of pleasure came from deep inside him. With a quick movement, he'd moved them so they were side by side, facing each other. He traced the delicate lines of her waist with his forefinger; her body was petite, but perfectly formed. His eyes clouded in a sexual haze, the lids heavy with desire. He swallowed a groan when he leaned down to take her breast into his mouth, rolling the nipple around his tongue. She arched her back, and a small moan came from her as she cupped the back of his neck, keeping him against her.

"So damn beautiful," he whispered against her skin.

Jarrod lifted his head and went on his knees. He smoothed his hands up and down her soft skin, slowly for his benefit, teasing himself with her beauty. He reached up and drew her panties down her slim legs. Jarrod heaved a deep breath in as his eyes were mesmerized by the blonde thatch between her luscious thighs. He opened her legs and leaned down a breath away from the pink, glistening artistry of her sex.

"Jarrod." She whispered his name.

He felt her fingers weave in the strands of his hair, trying to pull him closer, but he wanted to tease her a little longer. So he concentrated on her inner thighs, kissing each one. He moved closer until he was a breath away from tasting her. He couldn't help breathing in deeply; her scent was sexy as hell.

"Take your jeans off," Maisy said, tugging at the waistband.

He looked up and saw the desire burning in her eyes, her cheeks flushed, and her lips parted.

Fuck, he was never going to survive if he was naked.

"Please," she pleaded.

He stood up, toed his shoes off, then took his wallet from his pocket and set it on top of the nightstand before taking his jeans and boxers off simultaneously.

"Oh my," she breathed.

His heart nearly stopped, and he swallowed deeply when he saw the look in her eyes. But she wasn't looking at him; her gaze went below his waist. Quickly, he went back between her thighs, and without delay, he slipped a single finger inside her, his thumb parting the wet flesh.

"How's this?" he whispered.

She gasped then moaned as she clamped her muscles around his digit, which got wetter as he continued to move inside her. His erection strained and hurt with need. But he wanted her to feel pleasure more than he needed to feel his own.

She oozed sexiness. But, oh, so much more—more than just sex. Jarrod moved up her body, but continued to assault her wetness, massaging the hub of nerves that had her arching her back.

He was fascinated by her expression, and he slowly inserted another finger, the wetness of her desire apparent as she gasped and writhed against his hand. He kissed her hard, and she returned it just as fervently. He nuzzled his way down her neck until he reached her breasts.

She responded to his touch by moving her hips, and he caressed her nipples with his tongue. Maisy ran her hands over his shoulders, lifting herself to his touch, wanting whatever he was willing to give her.

"Oh God," she whispered as she widened her legs and pushed hard. Her back arched off the bed. "Jarrod, please, that's… I'm…" she panted.

Fuck, she was gorgeous, and knowing he had brought her to the heights of passion made him happy. He loved how she responded to his touch so quickly. Maisy's hips reacted to the tempo of his digits, and

Jarrod moved to give the other breast equal attention.

The scent of her passion reached his senses, and he breathed in deeply. "I can't wait to put my mouth where my fingers are," he said, hardly able to get the words out before she arched up hard.

Her mouth opened, but she didn't say a word, her eyes tightly shut. Her hands stretched behind her as she gripped the headboard, and her wetness drenched his fingers in a stream of desire as her body thrashed in what was the hottest thing he'd ever seen.

Jarrod wanted to wait for her to be still, but he knew he couldn't hold off any longer. He reached into the drawer at the side of the bed and retrieved a condom. He ripped the packet apart with his teeth, and it almost set him off when he rolled it on…carefully.

Jarrod looked at Maisy, and he smiled. It was the first time he'd seen her without that look of sadness, and he hadn't realized it until now.

"You are amazing," he said as he crawled back to cover her body with his own, settling in between her legs.

"No," she said, wrapping her arms around him, then resting her hands on his ass and squeezing it. "You are."

He enjoyed her touch on his skin, her fingertips squeezing his flesh as his muscles tightened, a natural reaction to her. She grabbed him, pulling him so close to her that his hard-on swelled even more… Shit, was that even possible? And when she wrapped her legs around him and stroked her way up his body until she cupped his face, drawing his head down for a kiss, it blew his mind.

The emotion behind the kiss was all-encapsulating right down to his soul. This wasn't just sex… *Is this what love is?* If it was, he felt no uneasiness at all. With Maisy, his happiness overtook any other emotion. Jeez, this woman made him want and do things he'd never needed before.

He positioned himself, lost all coherent thought as she pushed up, and thrust inside her. She was tight, and exquisite, and it made his breath ragged. He whispered over her lips words of encouragement and passionate, sexy endearments.

Their caresses were soft, then hard as he swept her up in an earth-shattering kiss. When their lips parted, they were both panting, and he met her gaze, the smoldering intensity almost making him drown in the intensity of the color.

They made sounds without words, noises of pure, animalistic pleasure. Jarrod withdrew slowly, watching her face, gauging the reaction to his movements. Maisy arched up, and met him in every thrust—the joy on her face shining.

Keeping the rhythm slow, he kissed her face, neck, shoulder, and then back up to her lips. Jarrod slipped a hand beneath her bottom, raising her, so penetration was deeper. And if the way her nails were sinking into his skin was anything to go by, she liked it.

He forced himself to slow down. But it was a struggle to hold on just that little bit longer, the need built in him causing a rising crescendo.

"Harder. Please, harder."

The break in her voice told him she was close, and he wanted her release more than he wanted his own. Jarrod did as she asked, and sank into her as far as he could.

"Yesssss!" she cried out.

The sound of her escalating cries spurred him on,

and suddenly he felt her clench around him, pressing her hips hard into his, and when they came it was in mutual surrender, the power behind their orgasms sending him into a shivering ecstasy as he thrust deeper and faster.

His release was hot and violent as she tightened around him. Her satisfaction met his thrust for thrust, moan for moan, in shuddering waves. He gathered her whole body tightly against him, and let his head fall into her neck, her skin as slick as his, panting out her breath as his lips pressed into the pulse at her nape.

****

Maisy felt warm and contented. She snuggled close to Jarrod after he returned from the bathroom and tightened his arm around her. Her head rested on his chest, and she felt his legs' hairs against hers' smoothness.

It was impossible to stop her tired body from getting even closer. She wanted to crawl inside him, and even that wouldn't be close enough. He was so loving, and it made her feel special.

Maisy hadn't done anything that made her this happy in a long time, and Jarrod made her feel that way. But she wasn't sure how long it would last.

"Hey, are you okay?" he asked as his fingers tilted her chin.

Maisy allowed her lips to touch the skin on his neck. Closing her eyes, she enjoyed the feel of him against her mouth, and used her tongue to taste him. A raw, earthy sound came from him, and she didn't deny him when he kissed her on the lips.

When they parted, both of them were breathless. Maisy trailed her fingers over his bristly jaw, loving the feel of the roughness against her skin. "I'm perfect," she said, answering his earlier query. "And you?"

"More than perfect. That was incredible. Better than I ever thought in my wildest dreams."

She felt his arms come around her, and didn't need any encouragement to allow him to hold her so tightly. The only thing she didn't like was the deep feeling in the pit of her stomach. Maisy wondered whether a world of pain would be heading her way, because this wasn't just sex. It had accumulated into emotions she'd never felt before.

Could she let her heart become so vulnerable when it already teetered precariously on the brink of the abyss?

"Stop it," Jarrod said as he leaned up on an elbow, looking down at her.

"What?" she said, looking up at him.

"Stop torturing yourself. You are allowed to be happy."

How did he do that? Get inside her head, and know what she was thinking?

"I don't want to forget," she said as tears rose behind her eyelashes.

"Oh, baby, you won't ever forget them." He laid his hand on her chest, over the location of her heart. "They are here, embedded inside your heart forever."

That made her cry. Maisy wrapped her arms around him and held on tight. He turned onto his back, drawing her with him so that she lay on top of him. His strong arms hugged her so close she could hardly breathe, but she didn't care.

Maisy was learning about the variability of her emotions. It confused her by what he asked about her feelings. She wanted it to be just sex. It wasn't, and she hadn't expected to feel so emotionally connected to him.

Oh, he understood her, he got that she was damaged—and he treated her as if she was precious.

Jarrod was willing to be patient with her, but for how long? And would she always feel guilty for being happy? Maisy knew the only way was to move on, but did she want to?

She looked at Jarrod as he ran a finger down her cheek, and a shiver of desire ran through her body. The pad was rough against her skin. He smoothed it along her collarbone and across to her earlobe before his hand cupped the side of her face. She moved into his gentleness.

"You're going to be okay, baby. I'll take care of you." His voice was hoarse, and she could have sworn there were tears in his eyes. Jarrod drew her head toward him. Kissing her with such gentleness, so full of emotion, it was almost as if…

No, she was reading too much into it. Wasn't she? She questioned her thoughts. Could he love her?

Holy cow, did she love him? Could she let her heart become vulnerable again after everything that had happened in her life? The pain…

"Stop it," Jarrod said as he searched her eyes.

"What?" She inclined her head further into the pillow to see his expression.

"Stop torturing yourself, and let whatever is going to happen take place in its own time." He was inside her head again, reading her. "You don't ever have to pretend with me, baby girl."

His tender attention was never far away, and his seeming need to protect her vibrated from him to her. The sweetness of his touch as he cupped her cheek overwhelmed her, and her breath lodged in her chest when she saw the sheer warmth in his eyes.

There was something in his expression just for a split second, and she frowned as she searched those gorgeous green eyes, but she couldn't read what he was trying to hide. Then he smiled lazily, the corners of his mouth lifting as his thumb stroked her bottom lip.

What would it be like to have a man like Jarrod in her life—not just for now, but forever? The hurt Jack had bestowed on her had been nothing compared to the loss of her children. Her heart was constantly in pain.

"Hey, are you all right?"

She nodded. "Yes, I'm more than all right. You make me feel good, magnificent."

"So, would you mind if I did this?"

And he positioned himself on top of her, and with one thrust he was inside her, and she let out a small cry. The look of horror on his face made her realize he'd mistaken her cry as one of pain when it had been a pleasure.

She gripped his arms as he began to pull himself out. "No! Again, harder—please."

The relief on his face was plain to see. The break in her voice was there even to Maisy's ears, and she pushed up to meet his hips, pressing hard. She wanted to feel him fully inside her.

Her orgasm came so quickly it shocked her as her inner walls rippled against him. He matched each spasm of her climax with his own. His head fell to her neck, and he bit her skin. A lusty feeling of warmth stole over her, and she seemed powerless to resist as her body lost itself entirely in the pleasure he gave her at every touch.

Every inch of her was tingling, and the flame of desire ignited in a ball of fire so intense that Maisy didn't want the flames to subside…she wanted to burn with desirous emotion that took her breath away. He was hard and hot and everything she'd never had before. It shocked her that she could feel this way.

She realized her eyes had closed, and when she opened them he was looking straight at her while still buried inside her. She couldn't help but press one more time into him. Her orgasm was so intense and powerful, like the one he'd just shouted out. God, she wanted this man so much.

Jarrod kissed her jaw, her neck, and she loved every second of his lips on her, the heat in his eyes almost singing to her, and certainly making her face heat up. He drew away from her, lay back, and took her with him, wrapping his strong arms around her. She hadn't felt so safe and secure for a long time.

"You are the only person I can be myself with. I don't have to pretend." Her fingers smoothed over his chest; the springy hair felt like silk.

"You better believe it, baby girl."

"I do," she whispered.

She leaned her head back to look up at him. He kissed her, which was warm and sensual, telling her they were by no means finished loving. It was fine by her.

"I want you, baby."

"You have me," he murmured.

"Jarrod?"

"Uh-huh?" He moved down her body, his lips setting fire to her skin.

He pushed her breasts together as his mouth went from one to the other, giving them equal amounts of attention. A surge of renewed longing—she didn't know where it came from—enveloped her body in a fire-driven desire.

"Can I make love to you?" she asked him in a voice only vaguely recognizable as her own.

Jarrod let his forehead drop to her chest. "Damn, I wasn't expecting that," he said as she felt the stubble of his unshaven jaw rub against her skin.

A quiver of excitement ran through her, and she felt his body tremble.

He looked up at her, hair all tousled, cheeks flushed, and eyes glazed. "Are you sure?"

"Oh yes. I'm sure." Maisy pushed him over and climbed on top of him.

His hands immediately cupped her ass, pulling her closer. She pulled them away and pushed them above his head. His body radiated a raw, primal strength that took her breath away, and his thighs parted so she fit perfectly into his body.

She stretched her body and lay entirely over him. His breath was ragged, his eyes dark with desire, and he watched her through thick, half-closed lashes.

Maisy smiled. She liked this, liked feeling naughty. She kissed his neck, loving the salty taste, and moved so she could wrap her lips around his distended nipples. As she scraped her teeth over the distended skin, she smiled at the ragged moan erupted from his chest.

He started to say something, but she sank to her knees, and the words were gone. He reached down and tangled his fingers in her hair. There was no pressure, his touch light, and gentle, but she could feel the discipline it took him not to push her head where he wanted it to go.

Licking her lips, she brushed them against his inner thigh, then to the other side, and his fingers tightened in her hair. Her tongue came out and licked up the length of his hardness. She was surprised by how silky the skin was, and she wrapped her hand around the base and felt his solid erection throb against her palm.

Maisy parted her lips and swirled her tongue around the tip, tasting the fluid that had seeped from him, and the taste excited her. Her heartbeat thwacked against her ribs as she closed her mouth around him, sliding up and down, taking him deep into her mouth. He was big, but that didn't deter her at all.

"Jesus, Maisy, you have to stop."

She frowned. Why? Why did she have to stop? Was she doing it wrong? She looked up at him, her lips just above the tip of his penis. He must have seen the question in her eyes because he put his hands under her arms and pulled her up.

"Honey, I want to be inside you when I come, and I'm precariously close. I love what you're doing, but it's for another time when I can control myself. Right now, you only have to touch me, and I'm like a rocket waiting to take off."

"Oh." She didn't know what else to say. She would have thought she'd be embarrassed by how expressive he was, but she wasn't.

He lifted her by the hips and brought her down to sit on him. He sank into her with one thrust. She was wet, making it so easy for him to slide in and out.

"That feels so good," she said as she met his thrust with the same urgency as his.

Jarrod shuddered, emitting a groan, and she put her hands on his shoulders as she drew him out, and then pressed him back in. She loved the lustful expression on his face, and she continued.

"That's it," he said as they built up a rhythm.

He brought his hands up to her breasts, cupping them as his thumbs rubbed against the skin. Their bodies fused in a shared passion for loving as she sat back and rested her hands behind her on his raised thighs. Lights started to flash behind her closed eyes, and he gazed at her intently when she opened them. She could feel her muscles gripping him tighter.

Jarrod drew her down and kissed her as she gripped the pillow behind him. With each sure stroke, she could feel herself getting to the edge, almost falling off, but not quite.

"Oh God, Maisy, you are so amazing, so damned gorgeous. Ahhhh, I'm so close. Are you ready, honey?"

She kissed him, swallowed his groans with her own, and their tongues fought a battle of desire and passion far beyond what she'd ever experienced.

"Yes, baby, yes, I'm ready," she cried out. "Now, Jarrod, now."

Their bodies shuddered as they bucked and thrashed against each other's shared release. The pure heat was like the sun exploding into a million shards of intensity. They rode each other until every last shuddering wave of desire slowed down. She collapsed on top of him, her breathing faster than she'd ever thought she could breathe.

They'd both been on a journey of such intense pleasure, the complete satisfaction she now felt exhausted her. As Jarrod slipped out of her, she stayed where she was, and strong arms tightened around her. There were no words, just a mutual soul-entwining moment that left them both speechless.

They lay wrapped in each other's arms, eventually

falling asleep. At some point during the night she felt him move her so she was on her back. Maisy woke and drew him close, opening her arms to enfold him against her warmth. He moved toward her without hesitation.

Chapter 12

As Jarrod started to kiss Maisy, she felt his lips taste her skin before he took her nipple into his mouth. His tongue did things to her nipples that made her almost stop breathing. This was the kind of passion that had been missing from her life.

It was only a moment, but the value of it was incomparable. How many people got to have a point in time they've been waiting a whole life for, and didn't know it, until it happened—*if* it happened?

No man had ever kissed her the way Jarrod did. No man had held her as if she was the most important thing in his life. He touched her heart and soul, and it was the most tender sensation she'd ever experienced.

He devoured her, and she loved it. She wanted him again, and again, and she didn't think the feeling would ever leave her.

"You're more beautiful than I imagined, and I thought that would be impossible." His voice was raw, and the wild need in his eyes as he looked up at her sent shivers down her spine.

His demeanor was hungry—hungry for her. That excited Maisy as she pushed her head back onto the pillows. His tongue moved down her belly, stopping at her navel.

Maisy reached behind her and held onto the wooden bed rail, the deep carving rough on her hands, but she didn't care. A flood of arousal heated her body until she was almost combustible, and it wouldn't take much for her to explode with the pleasure he was evoking inside her.

"Aah, Maisy, I knew you had hidden all that heat and passion. I just had to coax it out of you," he said as his hand went in between her legs. "You're so damned sexy." His voice was at least two octaves lower than average, and the sound of those words made her wetter against his fingers.

Without thought, her legs widened as far as physically possible, her limbs supple from yoga. His mouth was so close to where she wanted it that the anticipation was overwhelming. She looked down to find him staring right back at her, his eyes almost black with desire.

"Now, baby, shall I put my lips where you want them?"

"Yes, oh yes, please." Maisy needed it so badly it ached in the pit of her stomach. Even though they'd only just made love, the desire and the need to go over that edge felt like it was their first time.

She held her breath as his lips hovered above her clitoris, and his eyes never wavered from hers. Then she felt the softness of her flesh, his mouth swiping the hub of nerves, and she couldn't help but lift her hips to him as she pushed her head back.

He traced her folds with the hard tip of his tongue, drank at her wetness, teasing her, making her womb tighten so much it almost hurt.

"Please, Jarrod, please." Her hips matched the rhythm of his tongue; she couldn't have stopped if she'd tried.

"Are you ready, babe?" As he spoke, the hum of his lips nearly drove her mad.

"Yes, yes." Her voice rose higher than she'd ever heard, and she had no control over that, or anything else.

He pushed her legs back so she was completely open to him. He cupped the back of her calves, and she felt the rough scrape of his bristles against her inner thigh, which only heightened the fervor rampant inside her.

His tongue corresponded with her hip movements as his thumb slid over her, fueling the orgasm that built up a throbbing sensation where every single nerve quivered. It was there, teetering of the edge of the abyss, and she fisted both hands in the sheets. He groaned and touched her so erotically that lust shot through her at speed. She couldn't control it, and didn't want to.

She could feel the sweat on her body but didn't care; she didn't bloody care. Maisy accepted his touch as if it was the most natural thing in the world. The chemistry they had exclusive and incredible.

"God, Maisy." His face was flushed, and his eyes bright, lashes slightly lowered. "You have no idea what you do to me. I want you so much, all the time. I want to possess you, feel you. Did you know that?"

"I want you to do it, please." She begged for something that was driving her crazy with need.

The moment his lips surrounded her and his tongue entered her she cried out, bowing her back to meet his ravaging mouth. Her body writhed in pleasure as an orgasm sprinted through her senses, soaring to an almost unreachable height until she thought she might pass out with the pleasure.

Finally, it started to waver, and her breath and energy were at zero. She was almost unaware of Jarrod's gentleness in easing her hips back onto the bed. She'd never had such endless gratification that nearly rendered her brain dead.

Jarrod's hands slid up her hips, over her waist, just barely touching her breasts, before he cupped her face and gently kissed her.

"Have you any idea how beautiful you are? Nothing I ever thought about you has prepared me for such passion."

He kissed her again, and she could feel how hard he was; he'd forgone his pleasure so it could be all about her. She inhaled a deep breath before she opened her eyes to find him gazing down at her. She could still see desire etched into his pupils.

"I could stare at you all night," he said as she wrapped her arms around his neck for the kiss she lifted her head to meet. It was slow, sexy, and sensual, especially when he thrust his tongue against hers, sucking and stroking the flesh.

He turned on his back, taking her with him; they were hip to hip, chest to chest, lips to lips.

His hand slid between her legs, back inside her, and it wasn't long before her breaths were coming fast. She'd already had several powerful orgasms, surely there were no more. But she could feel that tingle in the pit of her stomach, her sex clenched against his fingers, and she was so wet. Inch by inch he went inside her, until she could stand it no longer and sat down hard on him.

There were no words to describe how she felt as they rocked each other. Leaning down, she kissed him on the lips. Jarrod took her hands into his, laying them above his head, so her breasts were close to his mouth. He took one nipple into his mouth and grazed the skin with his teeth.

"God, that's good," she whispered hoarsely.

"It's amazing. You are incredible." His words were croaky.

His hips thrust into her again and again as they took each other higher. With her lips on his, Maisy swallowed every sound of pleasure mingled melodiously. The tightening of her inner muscles tightened around him. And that was it—an orgasm ripped through her with the strength of a tidal wave.

Maisy could feel the pulse of Jarrod's release as he came inside her. With tongues tangling and hips still moving each time he pushed into her, she felt her sensitive skin prickle with excitement more and more. The heavy press of his body against hers was delicious and stole every thought or worry from her mind. He possessed her. She was his—not just her body, but her heart, and every kiss he gave her, every touch of his body, told her that.

As with the last orgasms she had with him, they went on forever and ever. The blast of sparkling lights lingered behind her eyelids as they started to come down from their high. The only sound in the room was their heavy breathing. She let her forehead fall into the crook of Jarrod's neck. He kissed the top of her head and wrapped his arms around her as she snuggled into his side.

They held each other tightly, their bodies as close as they could be, their hearts pounding against each other. Jarrod didn't speak, and neither did she. It seemed words were not necessary.

Outside, darkness had prevailed, and the air had cooled down somewhat. Even as she thought about the chill, Jarrod pulled the covers over them.

How did he do that? How did he know what she wanted before she did? Her eyelids started to close. Was she ready for this? She had a funny feeling it would not be easy to let this man disappear from her life.

Did she even want him to?

Chapter 13

Maisy woke up to the sound of the ocean. The window sat slightly ajar, and her nose caught the scent of the sweet-smelling Mexican petunias. She was facing the sunlight high in the sapphire blue sky. It looked like a beautiful day. She glanced at the clock on the bedside cabinet; it was eight o'clock.

She tried to roll onto her back, but a warm body behind her prevented it. It took her a second to remember she wasn't in her house or bed. Then, in a rush, last night came back to her, and her face heated at the memory.

"Morning, Maisy." Jarrod's voice breathed in her ear.

She loved waking up beside him; it made her heart overflow with warmth. "How did you know I was awake?" Maisy knew she'd hardly moved except for just trying to roll onto her back.

"By your breathing, it's soft, and wispy, and very sexy."

Warmth started to travel up her body at the huskiness of his voice, and the memory of last night. She never once in her life thought herself that interested in sex. But she seemed to match Jarrod's passion equally. The mere thought of the response he'd encouraged from her almost had her heart-stopping.

It wouldn't have been like that with any other man, not even her ex-husband. With Jarrod, it was extraordinary, and only this man could have made it so. He moved slightly to let her turn on her back while he leaned above her on his elbow. His half-opened eyes stared at her with an emotion she wasn't sure she recognized, or perhaps she just didn't want to. Maisy found it all so confusing, and when he leaned down and kissed her, it threw her emotions into the spin dryer.

"I'm sorry," he said.

She frowned. "Sorry for what?"

"We didn't use protection."

Shit, they hadn't. "I think we'll be all right. It should be okay when I'm at that time of the month."

"If it isn't, you have to let me know."

"I will." She wasn't sure…no, she was sure—she didn't want children, yet. "Last night was incredible," she said quietly.

"Yes, it was." His lips nuzzled her neck.

"It has never been that good for me," she said shyly.

"Never?" he asked. "Your husband must have been an idiot. My God, Maisy, you were unbelievable. You are one hot lady."

"Jack and I were young. He liked more experienced women, and I wasn't used to men."

"It's difficult when you're young. We don't always make the right decisions."

"He was older than me by five years."

"That doesn't seem like much, but it is."

Maisy nodded. She now wanted to know more about his past. They always seemed to be talking about her. "Your mum died, is that why you were in a children's home?"

She could tell from his expression that he didn't want to talk about it. He sat up with a hand to his neck as if he were racked with tension. She didn't say anything but sat up, and pushed the pillows behind her so when she leaned against them, she faced his back.

"Yeah." He swung his legs to the floor and picked up his boxers. Slipping them on, he stood and went to lean on the window frame.

His back stiffened as he folded his arms across his chest. Maisy wanted to wrap her arms around him, but she didn't and waited for him to continue.

He had a strong back, the muscles were solid. When Maisy looked closer, and saw scars on his left hip, and along the bottom of his back just above his boxers. He didn't look at her, but spoke tenderly.

"The marks on my back are cigarette burns. She used to take great delight in doing that. It seemed to amuse her."

She held in the gasp that was about to burst from her chest. "How old were you?"

"About six. It was one of the short times she was allowed to have me."

"So you were in and out of care?"

He shrugged. "Yeah. But when Mom died, I lived there permanently, until I was old enough to leave."

Maisy covered her mouth, but a breath still managed to escape. She got out of bed and reached for his discarded t-shirt. Slipping it on, she walked over and stood behind him, sliding her arms around his torso.

Jarrod reached around and hooked an arm around her neck, bringing Maisy close to his side. She leaned her head against that part of his chest where his heartbeat was slow and steady…comforting.

"That's where you met Liam and Max," she said to confirm what he'd already said. She remembered how the three of them were inseparable that summer.

"Yes, we were trouble, all wild, and with major attitude problems," he said.

She could feel his chest move as he chuckled. Maisy put her hand on his jaw and brought it around to face her. "You have no brothers or sisters?"

"No." He took her hand and turned it over, kissing the palm. Leaning down, he touched his forehead to hers, holding her as his free hand coasted up and down her spine.

"I'm sorry you had such a horrible childhood," she said as she tried to imagine what it must have been like for him. But she couldn't; her childhood had been great, and she felt guilty for that.

"Don't you dare," he said.

"What?" She pushed away from him just enough to see his face.

"Feel sorry for me."

"It's hard not to, Jarrod. Anyway, how did you know?"

"Because your body went all tense and your breathing changed."

"You're very sensitive to other people's feelings."

"Only yours," he said. "You were an only child too?"

"Yes, but I was very fortunate. My parents are lovely, and I adore them."

"That's nice."

"Yes, I miss them. But they are away for another three months on a cruise. They've been married for forty years."

"Wow, all that time with one person." He raised his eyebrows at her.

"They love each other very much and still hold hands when they go out." Her mind went back to their last phone conversation. "They wanted to come home for the court case, but I wouldn't let them. I had to work hard at convincing them I'd be okay."

"I'll come with you."

"Don't be silly. You've taken enough time off work already."

She felt him draw a deep breath in. He looked as if he was going to say something, and she waited. Then he kissed the top of her head and simply said, "We'll see."

She opened her mouth to speak, but when his lips touched hers and kissed her deeply, she forgot about it instantly. Maisy forgot about everything.

"Come on," he said. "Let's get dressed and see if we can get Elsa."

"Will there be someone there now?"

"If not, we'll wait until there is."

"I'm so excited about having her back." She was unsure about taking care of the pups, but it didn't deter her excitement.

"I know. You're like a little kid."

****

It was a gorgeous morning. The blue sky was almost faultless except for a single, cotton ball-shaped cloud floating across it. The sun beat down with a warning of how hot it would be. Pretty soon, there would be a chill in the air as the nights got darker, and Fall would be upon them.

Jarrod followed Maisy into the reception area of the veterinarian clinic, holding a large puppy carrier. He could tell how excited she was by her walk, the big smile on her face, and her sparkling eyes.

Maisy had blown his mind last night. She'd been amazing, and they'd been amazing together, but that hadn't surprised him. And yet their lives were entirely different; she'd had what he'd never had—a family, love, stability.

She had so turned him on that he had broken the one rule he'd always stood by…protection at all times. What if she was pregnant, how would he feel about that? At one time he would have been petrified of being committed to something as important as children. But he found that the idea of having a child was growing on him; with Maisy, it would be a token of their love for each other. He just wasn't sure if Maisy was ready for that.

He'd known fifteen years ago that they would be perfect together. There was vitality, a sheer presence. He could still see that teenage girl after all the pain she'd gone through. Her response to his touch, the pleasure he saw in her face still fixed in his mind, and the excitement of finally making love to her brought him the peace he'd never known.

Jarrod realized that this tiny person who had endured so much pain was stronger than any woman he'd ever known. So sweet and trusting. Even all the bad things that had happened in her life hadn't take any of that away. She'd given herself to him so willingly, and her pleasure had been his.

This was the first time he'd ever made love to a woman with so much adoration in his heart. It hadn't just been a desire, it was a commitment, something he'd never considered before he'd met Maisy. Her beauty inside and out made him smile, as did her ability to reach deeply into his heart, hugging it with every touch and sound she made in his arms.

Maisy chatted with Jenny, stroking the welcoming kitty who sat on a cushion on the countertop.

"Oh, look out," Jenny said as he reached around Maisy and tickled the kitty's chin.

He chuckled as the little thing brushed against his hand and picked her up.

"Told you, that cat is nothing but an outrageous flirt," Jenny said.

Maisy laughed as he brought the kitty close to his chest and petted her until she purred so loudly it vibrated against him.

Maisy gave the receptionist her debit card to pay the invoice for Elsa's care. Once the transaction was completed, she turned around to face him. "We're going to get her now," she said with a massive grin on her face.

He put the kitten back down on the cushion, and it mewed with a degree of displeasure.

"It's okay," Jarrod assured the cat with a further stroke. She stared at him for a second before curling up and closing her eyes.

He followed Maisy into the back, and he couldn't help it when his eyes kept straying to her adorable ass in jeans that looked as if they'd been painted on. Damn, he knew what that fine ass felt like in his hands. *Eyes ahead*, he chanted to himself as he felt the zipper of his jeans go tight.

He could hear a dog barking and instantly knew it was Elsa. So did Maisy; she went at a fast pace the rest of the way. The only thing stopping her from breaking into a sprint was Jenny in front of her.

Jenny opened the cage, and Elsa bounded toward Maisy with an exuberance that almost knocked her over.

Elsa seemed so much better than yesterday, and her joy was evident as she wagged her tail while being petted and loved.

"Good girl. I'm so happy to see you." Maisy buried her nose into Elsa's neck and let out a hum of appreciation. "So, mummy, are you ready to bring your babies home?"

"I think she is," Jenny said.

"They're so cute," Maisy said as they all stared down at the sleeping pups.

The male had a funny little mark on his nose, which was cute, and the female's paws were darker than the rest of her coat, but their eyes had not yet opened. They were fast asleep in Elsa's cage and hadn't even stirred when the dog moved to greet them.

"Yep, they sure are," Jenny agreed.

Elsa went to Jarrod right after Maisy made a fuss of her. He saw the look in Maisy's eyes and the tears behind them and knew it was because the dog had been on the same journey of despair and sadness. Finally, they were both beginning to come to terms with their losses.

"Hey, girl," he said as he went down on his haunches to pet her. He chuckled as her wet tongue licked his face. "Are you ready to come home?"

As if she understood, she returned to the kennel and lay beside her two pups. She would go nowhere without them. Her eyes were resolute, and as if to show her determination she curled around the sleeping pups, stating quite clearly *wherever I go, they go*.

"It's okay, honey," Maisy said. "They're coming too."

A loud bark and a slight wag of her bushy tail confirmed she was happy about this, and they all laughed.

"Chris would have been here, but he's out on a call. If there are any problems at all, just give us a call. You shouldn't have to do anything with her stitches, they are dissolvable. They should disappear in about seven to ten days."

"Okay. I have to say, and I'm a little nervous."

"Don't be," Jenny said. "Elsa will be a good mom. Her maternal instincts have already taken over. And besides, you have this guy to help you," she said as she took the carrier from Jarrod and put the puppies in gently with the blanket they had been lying on inside the cage.

Maisy looked uncertainly at him, and he took her hand and squeezed it tightly. His heart did a jump when she smiled up at him.

When he'd seen her walking along the beach with Elsa, there had been something about how she moved that he couldn't put his finger on. But then, he'd known all those years ago she was different. What was it? That he couldn't say, but there was something about how they clicked…like pen and paper, sun and moon, always and forever.

What he hadn't known when seeing her on that beach was the heartache she had endured Once he had, he was more than happy to give her space, to let her come to him. Although persuading her to move to his place while he remodeled her house had worked for him.

Maisy's eyes sparkled, and she looked so beautiful that he brought her close to him and kissed the top of her head. It felt like the most natural thing in the world to do. Jarrod breathed in her scent and frowned to himself. He had to come clean with her. At some point he'd have no choice, especially now since he needed her to be part of his life.

Jarrod just hoped it wouldn't ruin what they had. He knew how she felt about lies, but he also knew she'd had a bad experience with her ex-husband and his money. He was trying to make her see that in general, men weren't all like the jackass she married, money or not.

****

Maisy stared at herself in the mirror as she ran her fingers through her hair, still damp from her shower. She conceded she needed a haircut. It wasn't long, but it was starting to get a bit straggly, and she liked it short these days.

Initially, they'd been going to babysit so Dottie and Mike could go out. But her friend had texted her and asked if they would like to come to dinner instead. Maisy was looking forward to the evening, even though she knew Dottie was just being nosey. It made her laugh at the interest Dottie had in her love life.

Thinking back to the last fourteen months of her life, it amazed her how she had come this far after seeing no light at the end of the tunnel. Then gradually, the light started seeping through, and she started to regain some of her life, but there wasn't a day that went by when she didn't think about her heartache.

Maisy pulled on her jeans and t-shirt and slipped on her pink pumps with a smile on her face as she thought about the last few weeks. So much had happened. She'd met Jarrod, had Elsa and the pups she didn't know Elsa was expecting, and her little beach house was now being renovated by Jarrod, a man who had attached himself to her heart.

Elsa and her babies had settled in beautifully in the last twenty-four hours, and she hadn't wanted to leave them tonight. Dottie had been more than happy for Maisy to bring them with her, and they were taking the truck, so Elsa didn't have to walk.

Maisy walked through the short hallway to the kitchen doorway and watched as Jarrod lifted the puppies and placed them in the carrier under the watchful eye of Elsa. This tall, broad man with a heart as soft as Jello…it almost took her breath away at the sight of him speaking so softly to Elsa and making sure to give her attention even while he held one of her puppies. They had been pleased by how well Elsa had adapted to being a good mum, although Maisy wasn't surprised.

Jarrod was so good with them. Elsa loved him, and the relationship between the two had made Maisy's heart sing. Elsa had been so unhappy for such a long time that it was unbelievable to watch them forge a relationship.

Did it make her a bad person to have feelings for this man?

Was it so wrong to want to be happy?

Maisy felt sure she loved Jarrod.

Realizing she had forgotten her mobile, she turned and went back to her bedroom to get it. She paused for a moment to look out the window. The early evening of September started to darken, and the waves brushing against the sand were the only sound she could hear.

She breathed in deeply; there was nothing like the scent of the now cooling air that came from the water. And when you could smell the snapdragons prevalent in Jarrod's yard at the back of the house, which faced the ocean, it gave her such a sense of being settled, a place where she could feel happy.

Was it too soon to be involved?

Her breathing was even. She'd learned in yoga class

how her breathing would help with her anxieties when they became too much to handle. Absorbed in her thoughts she didn't realize Jarrod had come into the room until she felt his arms come around her from behind.

"What's wrong, honey?"

Maisy closed her eyes as the tenderness of his voice rode over her. Maisy covered her hands with his. A surge of desire hit her when Maisy felt the touch of his fingers on her skin beneath the hem of her top made her heart rate speed up.

"Everything is okay, baby," Jarrod said.

"I like that."

"What?"

"The soft, sexy tone of your voice when you say, *baby*."

His lips touched her neck, and she moved her head to the side almost without thought so he could have better access.

"Somehow, sometimes I think you're faking about being okay," he said.

"What makes you say that?"

"Because you are as tense as a tightly strung guitar string."

She laughed. "Great analogy." She leaned back against his hard body, and he tightened his hold on her.

"So?"

"What?"

"Don't do that, Maisy."

"Do what?" she asked, trying to act stupid but failing miserably because he could read her like a book.

"Don't withdraw into yourself. Stop feeling guilty for being happy." He turned around and lifted her chin so she could look up at him.

"I can't help it," she said, her voice quiet. "It doesn't seem...right...for me to feel this way."

"Aww, honey. A dreadful thing happened in your life—there are no words to describe what you've been through—but you can't live your life forever feeling like this. Do you think Tom and Beth would like to see their mom miserable for the rest of her life?"

The words she wanted to say stuck in her throat, so she nodded in agreement with him. She knew he was right, but it hurt like hell. Maisy feared her memories of them would disappear, that she would forget they were a part of her life.

"They shouldn't be a sad memory. You should remember the happy times, the joy and pleasure they brought you. But you should not feel guilty for being alive."

He cupped her face. She felt the roughness of his hands against her skin and took comfort in them.

"I'm so afraid of forgetting them," she said, with the tears in the back of her eyes just a blink away from falling down her cheeks.

"Honey, they will always be a part of you, inside your heart, close to you." He smiled. "It doesn't make you a bad mom to get on with your life. It says you are strong, caring, and have suffered enough."

"I hate him." She didn't like that feeling, it wasn't her, but she couldn't help it.

"Who, Jack?"

"Yes, and that makes me hate myself for having such feelings for the father of my children. I detest myself for allowing us to get into the car with him."

Jarrod took hold of both her hands and leaned down

so he was level with her eyes. "Listen to me, you have every right to feel like that. God, he had been drinking and must have known the risks."

"Yes, but I should have seen it. I knew what he was like, and I should have known Jack would never have given it up." She couldn't stop the tears, and they fell from her eyes. "It should have been me. Not my babies!"

The tears fell onto his hand as he held hers. He reached up and smoothed them away with his thumb.

"I cannot even begin to understand what you're going through. But I know that feeling hate for someone who caused the accident is natural. But I bet Jack is living a life sentence. Whatever the courts decide, he has to live with what he's done."

Maisy nodded. She'd had few regrets in her life, but marrying Jack was one of them. But if she hadn't, she would have never had the pleasure of her children, albeit for a short time. She'd rather have had that than never had them at all.

It was hard to assuage the guilt she felt and get past those feelings that had been dominant in her mind for nearly fourteen months. Even the impending court case had no meaning anymore. Jarrod was right. Jack would have to live with his guilt forever, and no jail time could ever be as hard as that.

Suddenly she didn't care about making him pay—he would always have to live with what he'd done.

Maisy leaned in and let her head fall to Jarrod's chest. He immediately wrapped his arms around her, drawing her closer to him. His warmth spread over Maisy, and closing her eyes, enjoying the moment and his essence, which touched her senses.

"Do you think you can move on?" Jarrod asked.

His fingers caressed her back, making her feel secure and comforted. She looked at him, startled by his serious expression. But she knew he was only concerned for her, that he wanted her to be able to move on. And she could, now. Yes, she could do it.

"Yes, I think I can. I've been so happy since we met again. You've helped me more than I can ever tell you."

He smiled. "No, you've done it all yourself. I just came along at the right time. I'm glad to see that lovely smile of yours." He touched her lips with his.

He started to move back, but Maisy put her hands on his shoulders, reached up, and kissed him. His lips were soft and tender. She loved his taste, the texture, and the way he responded to her was a real confidence booster.

"Thank you," she whispered.

"I don't need your thanks. To see you smile and watch the sadness disappear from your eyes is enough."

It unsettled her sometimes how he understood her so well. She'd never had that with Jack. But Jarrod seemed to be in tune with her feelings and desires.

His hand dropped to her bottom. She could feel his erection, which sent a wave of excitement washing over her entire body. He leaned down and kissed her, an open-mouthed, all-encompassing kiss so delicious that her desire went from zero to a hundred in one second flat.

By the time their lips parted, Jarrod had lifted her off her feet, and she wrapped her legs around him. How that happened, she couldn't even remember. Both of them were breathing heavily.

"I suppose we do have to go out tonight?"

She nodded. "It will be nice for us to go out."

"It will; it's just that I can think of something nicer I'd like to be doing."

"Later," she said seductively.

"I'll hold you to that," he said as his hand squeezed her ass.

"I'm hoping that's a certainty," she said, chuckling, loving the sexy banter.

From the doorway came a bark. Jarrod turned around while she was still in his arms. Elsa looked fed up, as if to say, " Come on, *you two, hurry up.*

They laughed, and Jarrod let Maisy down and took hold of her hand, threading his fingers through hers. "Come on. The quicker we get there, the sooner we can come home, and I can get you into bed."

"Definitely," she said, feeling the same way.

****

The dinner Dottie cooked was delicious and the conversation entertaining, but Maisy wouldn't have expected anything less from her friend. She was a natural charmer, making everyone feel at ease and comfortable.

Mike and Jarrod already knew each other and seemed to have much in common. They took Elsa out for a walk while Maisy and Dottie sat talking in their lounge with a puppy each on their knees.

"Does Sam always sleep so well?"

Dottie nodded. "Yes, he's always been good at night."

"Gosh, you are so lucky. Tom was a nightmare. He had colic, which was exhausting, and Beth didn't like her cot, so she was always trying to climb out of it." Maisy smiled at the memory and saw the sadness on Dottie's face. "Please, don't be sad," she said as she stroked the sleeping puppy. "They are good memories; they really are."

"Are you sure, Maisy? Although you do seem

different you are positively radiant." She raised her eyebrow. "Has this got anything to do with Jarrod?"

Maisy thought about their nights together, and images of what they'd been doing together flashed through her mind. Her face became scorching.

"Maisy Fields, are you blushing?" Dottie said, chuckling.

"Oh my God." She put her hands up to her heated cheeks. "I feel like a teenager." She laughed.

"Come on then, spill the beans."

"Jarrod is incredible!" She couldn't contain her excitement. "I've never before felt anything like it in my life." She frowned, and Dottie quickly picked up on her facial expression.

"And, let me guess, you feel guilty?"

Maisy leaned back on the soft leather sofa and lifted the puppy close to her chest so she could cuddle him more. "Yes." She sighed. "It doesn't seem right for me to be so happy."

Dottie, sitting opposite her, pulled her legs up onto the chair and sat yoga-style. She settled the puppy in the crook of her arms and stroked her head before looking back at Maisy.

"What happened to you was a tragedy; there is no way I could ever imagine the horror of what you went through. But you deserve to be happy, and you, of all people, know that we can never take life for granted. It's a gift. Being happy is hard and isn't always easy or perfect. But you need to grab it with both hands and enjoy it."

"I can't explain what it is between us. Jarrod seems to get me and knows what to say. And the chemistry is there."

"It's rare to have a connection like you two seem to have. Good sex makes you glow," Dottie said, laughing.

Maisy couldn't help the smile that spread across her face. She pondered for a moment because it wasn't just the sex that made her feel good. It was Jarrod and what they had together; she hadn't thought she'd ever find that. Her experience with men had not been the best, and to enjoy the company of a man was exciting.

"You're right. I feel like a million dollars when I'm with him."

"Is it serious?"

She sighed. "I don't honestly know. I'm not sure how Jarrod feels or if he wants us to have something more."

"Honey, you need to ask him flat-out."

Maisy pursed her lips. "I know. But frankly, I'm happy to see where this takes us. I mean, why spoil a good thing by becoming too serious? And it's so good. But there is so much going on in my life."

"You're thinking about the court case?"

She nodded. "I think that before I move on, I need closure, although it doesn't seem so important now." Maisy frowned. "I hate Jack, and that's never going to change. But I think he must hate himself more, which is his life sentence."

"I agree. Being responsible for the death of your children is not something that one could ever forget. But what have you got to lose by being happy with Jarrod?"

"My heart."

"Perhaps. But unfortunately, life throws us these curves. And if you never put yourself out there, how are you ever going to move on?" Her brows knitted together as she pushed her thick bangs to one side. "Why not live for the day, grab what you can, and if it leads to a future, that's how it's meant to be."

"I want to be happy, and I am when I'm with Jarrod, but what if he just feels sorry for me?"

"Oh my God, Maisy, what a load of BS. You only have to see you two together; it's enough to make me want to grab my husband and have sex with him. You two are on fire."

"Damn, Dottie, do you love to see me blush?"

A loud laugh woke the pup up. His eyes weren't open yet, and Dottie gently patted him like a baby. "Go back to sleep, little one," she said in a soft, cooing voice as she leaned down and kissed the top of its head. "You need to name these pups."

"Yes, I know." Maisy sighed because she couldn't decide. Elsa had been such a poignant part of her life, of her children's lives, that she wanted it to matter.

She picked up the sleeping puppy and looked at his adorable face. His cute little pink nose twitched in his sleep, and his fat tummy felt squidgy in her hands. How could anyone not love such cuteness?

"Hey, it will all work out, you'll see," Dottie said. "Everything will come together as it should. Just…don't fight it, huh?"

"Yeah, court case and then work out where I'm going."

Dottie nodded. "That sounds like a plan to me, girlfriend."

Maisy narrowed her eyes. What had seemed important to her before wasn't now. The court case made Jack pay for what he did…all seemed inconsequential. His life sentence started when he crashed his car and killed their two children.

Chapter 14

Jarrod stood at the doorway and watched the two women as they cuddled the pups. He couldn't help but think about a life he now knew he wanted—one with Maisy, a future, a life with her.

His heart hammered in his chest. God, she didn't even know how beautiful she was. She kept the sadness that had occurred in her life hidden from others, but he knew it was there all the time.

"The pups slept the whole time," she said as Elsa came to see where her pups were. "I think we should hand these back to their mom. Although I don't want to. They're so cute."

Dottie laughed. "They certainly are." She stood up and reached over for the one on Maisy's lap. "Come on, Mom, let's settle you on your cushions."

Maisy stood up and faced him; she was so fucking gorgeous she took his breath away. Sometimes he felt as though he needed an anchor just to stop him from picking her up off her feet and carrying her anywhere he could to make love to her, or just hug, cuddle, or talk while holding hands.

Jarrod was aware he had no control at all with this woman, and he could feel his mind turning to complete mush. He knew Liam and Max would be laughing their heads off if they could see him now.

"Hey." She smiled. "Did you enjoy your walk?"

Dilys J Carnie

"I did, but Elsa was impatient to get back, and it looks like there's a storm on the way."

"Really?"

"I think we'll just make it home before it rains." Home...that sounded so right, especially with Maisy.

Their gazes locked on each other, and Maisy shoved her hands into her jeans pockets, blushing profusely. He loved that about her; she couldn't hide what she was thinking, making him as horny as hell. He wanted to pick her up, throw her over his shoulder, and take her to bed.

"Hey, you two, get a room."

He snapped out of his lust-filled thoughts and heard Dottie chuckle as she entered the room with Mike, carrying the puppies in their carrier. Elsa followed closely behind him.

"We thought you might want to go home now with the storm coming. But I can see that it might be more than the storm..." There was a teasing tone to Dottie's voice, and she had a look in her eyes that almost made him blush.

Jarrod cleared his throat and regained a little of his composure. He wasn't sure if he would ever not be mesmerized. Maisy filled his mind and body with a great need that heat radiated through his chest.

"Could turn into a Nor'easter according to the weather forecast," Dottie said. "God, I hope we don't lose power again."

"That's the downside of living by the ocean. When there's a storm, you know about it." Mike handed the carrier over to Jarrod.

Elsa stood by his side as he took hold of the two pups still sound asleep.

"You haven't been here through a storm yet, have

226

you, Maisy?" Mike said.

"No, but something tells me I'm going to find out exactly what a storm on Nags Beach is like."

"You better believe it," Dottie said.

"Come on then, let's get home."

"Thanks for tonight. It was nice." Maisy hugged her friend.

Jarrod took Mike's extended hand. "Thanks, buddy. Our turn next time, and bring the baby, that way, you don't need a sitter."

"I look forward to it. But I'm not sure you'll have us back again if we bring the baby." Mike laughed.

Dottie nudged her husband playfully. "Maisy loves him, and he's not that bad," she said laughingly but then changed her mind. "Perhaps a little boisterous."

"He's adorable," Maisy said. "And you'd better bring him."

"On your head be it," he said to Maisy with a grin before turning to Jarrod. "We need to meet with you at your office to discuss the new hotels on the coast. I wouldn't trust any firm but yours to do my work."

Fuck!

Maisy looked in his direction and frowned. She looked as if she wanted to say something but then thought better of it. She turned and headed for the door, and he followed, carrying the carrier.

"Sorry about that," Mike said quietly as he followed behind.

"No worries, bud. It's not your fault. I'm a complete jackass."

"Yes," Dottie said, "that describes you to a T."

Jarrod stopped in the doorway and looked at the couple they'd just spent a happy evening with . Mike raised his eyebrows. "I'm not going to argue with her," he said as he pulled Dottie to his side.

"You had better fix it," Dottie said to him. "She doesn't deserve any more unhappiness in her life."

"I know, and I am going to fix it," Jarrod said with more conviction than he felt. He may not be able to undo what he'd done, but he'd give a damn good go at trying to get her to understand. "I'll be in touch," he said. "Thanks again for tonight."

He looked up at the sky as he strode across to where Maisy had opened the car door for Elsa to jump into the back seat. *The sky isn't the only thing that looks angry*, he thought as he caught her eye for a second before she looked away.

He positioned the carrier beside Elsa and got into the driver's side. Fastening his seatbelt while he started the truck, he looked at Maisy. The tension in the air was palpable to say the least.

"Maisy—"

"Why didn't you tell me?" she interrupted him. "Why was it so important for you to lie to me?"

He frowned. To be honest he had asked himself the same question many times.

"It was stupid, and I regretted it from the very beginning. But I wanted you to like me for *me*, and when I heard your ex-husband had been with you, I didn't want you to think I was like him."

"But don't you see, Jarrod. You have done the same as he did. For different reasons, but still the same context."

Jarrod wanted to defend himself, but he didn't think it would make any difference. Her anger simmered, and he could see the hurt in her eyes. Maisy didn't speak for what seemed like minutes, but it was only seconds as she stared out the windshield.

"Let's go," she said without looking at him.

The clouds had been getting darker and darker as they had sat there. Jarrod would have liked to talk more, but he realized they needed to get home before the rain started. Maisy didn't say another word during the drive to his house.

When they arrived, he got the carrier out of the back seat and followed Maisy to the door, Elsa walking by at her side. They only made it inside when the heavens opened and the rain fell hard.

They didn't speak at all as they busied settling the pups down and feeding Elsa. He brought in all the outside furniture that wasn't tacked down. He usually wouldn't have bothered, but it looked like it could be worse than an average storm. He was soaked when he completed the task and locked the doors. He grabbed a towel from the kitchen and rubbed his face and hair.

Thunder gave its first roar, the noise overpowering. Jarrod expected to find Maisy sitting on the sofa, but she wasn't there. He saw her shoes sitting by the door where she had taken them off.

He threw the towel onto the countertop and walked through the short hallway to the bedroom. The door stood ajar, and he pushed it open to see Maisy standing facing the window.

Her back was straight as a rod, her shoulders tense. Had he blown it? He was such a stupid dick. The best thing that had ever happened to him was when she walked back into his life, and he'd done the one thing she hated—he'd lied to her.

Maisy turned around. He remained standing in the

doorway and shoved his hands into his jeans pockets because he didn't know what to do with them. Damn, he was nervous. *Fuck.*

She stared back at him, her thoughts hidden, her eyes calm and distant. But he could tell she was pissed off by her stance.

"You're soaked," Maisy said, moving toward him.

She stopped right in front of him, so close she had to look up at him. His wet hair dripped onto his already wet shirt. He should have changed into something dry, but he hadn't wanted to delay talking to Maisy any longer than necessary.

She fidgeted with her hands, apparently not happy with him. That much was evident in her eyes, and he couldn't blame her.

He decided to take a chance. What the hell did he have to lose? He took his hands out of his pockets and rested one on her hip, the other on the side of her neck.

"I'm angry with you, Jarrod. Why did you lie to me? Why not tell me you owned the business?"

"I was going to, but it never seemed the right time."

"All those conversations we had about my life, about us—and you never thought that was an important part of your life to tell me? That you're the boss and not what you pretended to be? That you owned the company, I thought you were an employee? It all makes sense now." Her tone was one of astonishment.

He felt a heavy weight pulling at his heart. "What do you mean *pretended to be*?"

"Oh, come on, Jarrod. You came across as just a simple guy who loved his job and loved to work with wood."

"I am that guy. Just because I own the company

doesn't mean I'm anything other than that…a simple man who loves what he does."

"You lied to me, making me wonder if I know you at all."

Maisy stepped back a little, but he didn't let her go, merely moved with her. She stood straight, and her body stiffened beneath his hands.

"Why, Jarrod? Why did you lie?"

"To begin with, I wanted you to see me and not what I had. And then when you told me about Jack and what he'd done by deceiving you about his money…well, it got harder to say anything."

"Oh my God, do you think I'm so shallow that I wanted your money?" Her voice went up a level as she stared at him in disbelief. "Do you honestly think I care about how much money you have?"

Maisy looked at him with horror and disappointment in her eyes, and it almost broke his heart. She gripped her hands in front of him so tightly he could see the white of her knuckles, and he felt his heart beating hard and fast.

"Do you have that opinion of me?" she whispered.

He grasped her hands and covered them with his own. "God, no, Maisy!" He was shocked she even thought that. "I don't believe that at all! You have to trust me when I say I know it was a stupid thing to do. It was complicated, and I didn't want it coming between us. The thought of losing you when I'd only just found you…" He shrugged his shoulders, his movement jerky as a tremor gripped his chest. "I couldn't bear the thought that I might lose you before we had a chance."

"Do you think I'm so pretentious that it would make a difference if you had money?"

"I guess I didn't think," he said as he settled his

hands on the side of her head and cupped her cheeks. It was a gesture that very well might get him slapped, but he was willing to take the chance. "Do you forgive me?"

He examined her eyes for a sign she did. His heart was racing and so loud that he thought she would probably hear it as it reverberated in his ears. Jarrod waited and watched as she searched his face. It was as if she was trying to decide whether she would forgive him for lying to her. He couldn't tell from her expression what she was thinking. Maisy's eyes were covered in a veil of blankness. Then she smiled, and he breathed a breath he had no idea he was holding.

"I learned a hard lesson when my kids died. Life is concise, so grab each day as if it was your last. So yes, I do forgive you."

Without warning, she went on tiptoes, and he bent lower to meet her in a kiss that held promise, that overwhelmed him with warmth and forgiveness—before turning into something that made his cold, wet body almost steam. He wrapped his arms around her. He knew she would get wet, but that was the furthest thing from his mind. Besides, she didn't seem to care as she pushed him so that his back felt the hardness of the doorframe.

Heat exploded inside him, warming him inside and out. Jarrod ran his hands down the sides of her body, his fingers lightly brushing the sides of her breasts, then her hips and thighs. Very slowly and deliberately, he touched every curve sensually.

They parted, gasping for breath. Jarrod looked at her for a short beat, trying to gauge how she may be feeling. He hated the thought of losing her through his stupidity. But her eyes had become bluer than he'd ever seen. She arched her brow at him.

"Are you sure we don't need to talk about this some more? Because if we do, we should stop now," Jarrod said.

"About lying?"

He flinched. "Yes."

"No, honey, we don't. It would have been better if you had told me from the beginning. And I kinda understand that after hearing about my ex-husband, you thought I might decide that you were both the same. But you are nothing like him." She smiled. "And besides, I can't possibly stay cross at you for long."

God, he was so relieved. It felt as though a weight had lifted from his shoulders. Maisy stood back and raised her arms, slipping off her top. Her pale pink satin bra showed off her little cleavage, and somehow the noise of the storm outside faded.

His attention had been fully gained, and he stood mesmerized when she pulled the zipper of her jeans down and stepped out of them. He looked at her barely-there matching pink panties and almost self-combusted when he saw a wet patch at the front of them.

She was wet for him. Jarrod shuddered and took a deep breath, hoping he could at least get his pants off before he got too excited. It made no difference that he'd seen her like this before. He didn't think he would ever get tired of seeing her just like this.

When she hooked her thumbs inside the elastic, slipped the silk down her legs, and stepped out of them, he had to take a few more deep breaths. He could hardly tear his eyes away from the thatch of blonde hair that covered her sex until she took off her bra; her rosy red nipples were hard, and the skin around them pebbled.

"Maisy." His voice was gruff.

"Yes," she whispered.

Jarrod swallowed. "Damn, you're gorgeous." He could feel his erection painfully tenting behind the zipper of his jeans

"Promise me, Jarrod, you will never lie to me again."

"I promise." The words were the easiest he'd ever uttered, but the wobble in his voice was uncontrollable, and he had to take a big gulp of breath at her beauty.

He slid his hands up her ribs, his thumb rubbing the hardened nipples. She let her head fall back as her mouth opened to let a gasp out. Jarrod couldn't resist what was offered and tasted the soft, silky skin.

"I think someone is very much overdressed." And to prove it she undid the button on his jeans and drew his zipper down very carefully.

The glaze in her eyes ruined him, and he shoved them down himself, toeing off his shoes carelessly. It was almost a disaster when they both tried to undo the buttons of his shirt, and they were on the verge of popping them off impatiently.

Maisy stood back slightly. "You have an amazing body, Jarrod," she said as her hands touched his abs, and he clenched them. It was a movement he couldn't help.

She smoothed her fingers over the indentations. Jarrod leaned back against the doorway and closed his eyes as she moved further and further down his body until she stopped just at the base of his hardness. He reached behind him to hold onto something and gripped the doorframe as she went to her knees.

"Jeez, Maisy, I don't know if I can last long."

"I don't want you to, baby. I want you to relax and enjoy."

Maisy reached out, her fingertips barely touching skin. But it was enough for him to grit his teeth…and then she wrapped her hand around his sex. They both groaned when she started to rub up and down in slow strokes. He threw his head back with an abandonment he'd never felt before.

Oh, fuck, he was going to lose it, and that was profound in its entirety. When he felt her lips go around him he nearly shot off the ground. They were soft and warm; the texture of her tongue stroking him made his heart almost jump out of his heaving chest.

"Maisy, that's so good."

She licked him as if it was her favorite ice cream. He put his hands in her hair; he wanted this so much, but he wanted her more. He needed to be inside her. A ringing in his ears told him he was close—really close—and he couldn't help the involuntary movements his hips were making.

"Maisy, ahh baby, you have to stop now."

He lifted her up in her arms. She wrapped her legs around him and braced her hands on his shoulders as he turned and leaned her against the wall.

"Did I do something wrong?" she asked.

"God no, honey. You did everything right." He saw her frown. "What you just did was amazing, and I loved it, but that's for another time."

Jarrod gripped her bottom, lifting her higher so she was right against him. He ground his hips against her, oblivious to the storm outside, to anything other than the two of them.

Jarrod felt her wetness slide against his erection, and he kissed her hard, unable to stop the groan that came straight from his chest. He left her mouth to taste her throat, and she let him have access by leaning her head back, mouth open and eyes closed. She had never looked more beautiful than she did at that moment.

"Jarrod," she gasped out.

He lifted her higher so he could place his mouth over the hardness of her nipples. Oh God, she was so fucking perfect.

She gripped him with her thighs. At this rate, he wouldn't last long enough to get inside her. Maisy had been through hell and back, and he always wanted to give her the attention she deserved, but he was so full of desire for her he couldn't stop himself.

"Jarrod, honey." She smoothed a hand over his damp hair and hugged him. "You don't have to be gentle with me all the time. I want you. I want you soft, sweet, and loving, but I also want hard and fast." She smiled. "I'm not a porcelain doll."

She kissed his ear, bit the lobe, and lowered her hand between them. Holding his straining hardness, she positioned him at her opening, and he looked at her for a second before pushing in as far as he could go. It was pure heaven.

His lungs compacted until he thought they would squeeze all breath from him. He lifted Maisy's hands above her head and held them there with one hand while his other gripped her ass. Jarrod met her glittering gaze and moved his hips, watching as her eyes closed. A hum came from her chest.

He did it again, slow, deliberate…until he felt himself wanting to go harder, and harder, until he was so deep inside her it seemed impossible to tell they were two bodies and not one.

"Faster, baby. Faster and harder." Her voice was

almost unrecognizable as she breathed out those words with his hips doing just as she'd asked. She wrapped her legs around him tighter, and he let go of her hands so she could put them around his neck.

Jarrod closed his eyes. Their bodies were slick with sweat, and he could feel her lips on his neck, sucking on the skin. "Kiss me," he said to her.

Maisy did just that, and immediately their tongues tangled. "Jarrod," she moaned. "I'm coming, don't stop, please don't stop."

"I'm not stopping. Come for me, baby."

And he felt the way her insides clenched him, the feel of her heartbeat as it pounded against his chest. She closed her eyes though he wanted to see them, and he whispered for her to open them as his orgasm started. They came together, draining each other of every single emotion they had.

Watching, trying to anticipate each other's needs, they trembled at the great height at which their lovemaking had completely encompassed anything he had experienced.

"I can't even put into words what that was like," she whispered as she let her head fall onto his shoulder.

Jarrod could feel her body going slack, and he took them both over to the bed and lay down, keeping his arms around her as she fell asleep. His own eyes drifted shut, and he smiled as he kissed the top of her head.

****

Jarrod awoke to the sound of rain on the window, and he reached out to the spot next to him, but it was empty. Sitting up, he ran his fingers through his hair as he swung his legs over the side of the bed. Picking up his jeans from the floor, he pulled them on, and without fastening them he went to find Maisy.

The pups were asleep in the corner, but there was no sign of Elsa or Maisy. He carried on through the kitchen into the living room. She stood looking out the large bay window with Elsa at her feet.

Jarrod's heart executed a little somersault inside his chest; she looked so alone…just one woman and her dog. He went behind her, put his arms around her waist, and pressed a kiss to her neck.

"You okay?"

She nodded and wrapped her arms over his.

He pulled her in closer, letting his lips brush her cheek. "I missed you."

She laughed. "I only left you moments ago."

"Too much time," he said.

"Hmm." She wiggled her butt against him. "I can feel exactly how much you miss me."

"I want you," he said, chuckling at her directness.

"I think I'd already deduced that." He chuckled.

Maisy turned around in the circle of his arms. She smiled at him, cupped his face in her hands, and went on tiptoe to kiss him on the lips. It was soft and gentle, and his heart gave a little hop at the sweetness of it.

"You know I trust you," she whispered.

He didn't answer for a second; he couldn't because his lips were kissing her. "I'm glad you do, honey." He leaned back slightly. "Maisy." He cupped her face, and those beautiful blue eyes, so open to him, looked sad. "You're upset?" He thought about last night and frowned; he couldn't think why she was so upset. "With me?"

"No, baby, not with you. With myself."

"Why?" He used his thumbs to smooth her cheek.

"Maisy." He took her hand and led her to the sofa. Sitting down, he pulled her, so she landed on his knee, his arms around her, hopefully comforting. "Tell me what's wrong."

Elsa came over as if to make sure she was okay, and then with a look that Jarrod could swear was one of consternation, she disappeared. Jarrod looked at Maisy's face. She smiled, but it didn't reach her eyes. He had a niggling feeling that something was up.

"Did I hurt you?"

"No, baby." She leaned forward and kissed his jaw. "You didn't hurt me."

When her lips touched his skin, he breathed again. He hadn't realized he'd been holding it in, waiting for her to answer.

"Then what is it?" he asked, his voice low, but with a lump stuck in there. He couldn't speak any louder.

For a moment, she looked toward the window without speaking. Jarrod had one arm around her back, holding her close. Picking up her hand, Jarrod kept it inside his. Maisy had a sharp mind, but she wasn't always confident in her feelings, so he didn't say a word, just waited for her.

She cleared her throat, and continued looking out the window, refusing to meet his gaze. Jarrod could never remember sharing a moment like this with any woman where he wanted to know her thoughts. He guessed this is what one did when in love. No—this was what he wanted to do for Maisy.

Every facet of her enthralled him to his very being. There was nothing about her that he didn't love. All he wanted was to see her happy, relaxed, and finally having someone in her life to trust, and look after her the way she should be.

"I've never said thank you to you, Jarrod."

Even now, when she said his name, his heartbeat accelerated, and his body throbbed.

"For what?" He frowned.

"Taking good care of me."

"It's not necessary. I didn't do anything."

She sent him a smile. "It is important to me."

Was it wrong that all he wanted to do was breathe in her feminine, musky scent, and pick her up to take her to bed? He would never tire of her slender legs wrapped around his hips, his body close, hers open and compliant as they satisfied each other entirely.

Jarrod turned her palm over and laced his fingers with hers. Even her tan was light against his; her hands were so small, dainty. Everything about her so very neatly packed together, his desire for her was off the wall.

The rain was still coming down with a vengeance, but it wasn't cold, and the air conditioner kept the humidity at bay. There were streaks of lightning crossing the sky after loud sounds of thunder. He had thought the pups might be frightened, but when he'd last passed them, they were fast asleep.

"Since I've moved to the beach house and met you, I seem to think of them less. I haven't even finished the painting I was doing of them."

"Is that what's under the cover on the easel?"

She nodded.

"You'll finish it when you're ready. Painting your children is a journey; as you brush each stroke, it's another moment to keep in your memory. Maybe you haven't finished because you're frightened it will be the end of the memories of the time you had with them?"

"That's exactly it. Oh, Jarrod, I couldn't have said how I feel any better than that. How do you do that? How do you always know what I'm feeling?"

"I don't. I think we are on a level where our relationship lets us understand each other completely. But that's not the whole story, is it?"

Maisy shook her head. "No."

He kissed her because he couldn't resist anymore. She returned it with a vigor that made him want to carry her back to bed there and then. But he forced himself not to; she needed to get whatever was worrying her off her chest.

"That was enjoyable," she whispered breathlessly.

He smiled. "It was more than nice."

She laughed, then suddenly the smile disappeared. "Jack is being sentenced next week."

"Yeah," he said. "And I'm going with you. And don't even think about saying no."

"I don't want to go."

"Honey?" He turned her face to look at him. "You have to go."

"I know. It's just...I don't have that same hate for Jack now. I feel sorry that he'll have to live with what he's done for the rest of his life. So it makes no difference to me whether he goes to prison or not—it won't bring Tom and Beth back to me."

He drew her closer as he leaned back on the sofa, and she lay her head on his chest.

"We will do this together. You'll never be on your own. I'll always be here for you."

Maisy lifted her head, and he saw in those eyes what he'd been waiting for since the first time he set eyes on her all those years ago. He saw love, and his heart filled with happiness he'd never experienced.

"I love you, Jarrod Steel."

He breathed in and closed his eyes before breathing out again, looking at her. She smiled.

"I love you too." He lifted her, and she automatically wrapped her legs and arms around him. He squeezed her bottom, and that action drew her closer. "This is going to be great, we are going to be great," he said.

She kissed him long and hard, and he felt himself get harder. Her lips tasted sweet and sexy at the same time.

"Without you I would have never been able to come to terms with all of this."

He wrapped his arms around her and leaned his forehead against hers. "I love you, Maisy. We will make happy memories, but you'll never forget the memories of Beth and Tom."

"No," she whispered, "I won't."

Epilogue

Maisy couldn't contain her excitement at Jarrod returning home after nearly a week away. It seemed to take forever for Friday, even though they'd spoken on the phone twice a day.

She wasn't sure how he was going to react to her news. To begin with, Maisy hadn't been sure about her feelings regarding what she had discovered this morning. But once she'd thought about it and what it meant to her, she couldn't wait to tell him.

The nights were drawing in, and the end of November was close. She curled her legs up and leaned back on the sofa. Tiredness overtook her, but she thought that might have something to do with her news and the excitement she felt. Elsa jumped up onto the couch to sit by her, and she stroked the dog's soft hair.

She'd kept both pups and had finally named them. The female was called Anna from a character in *Frozen*, and Beth had loved that film. The male one they had named David in memory of Tom, who loved David Beckham, the footballer.

"Hey, Elsa," she said as the dog pushed her nose against her hand. She threaded her fingers into the long, golden coat, and Elsa settled her head on Maisy's lap.

The court case had been traumatic, but Jarrod stood by her, holding her hand tightly the whole way through the sentencing. No amount of pleading from his lawyer had got Jack less than he deserved.

Dangerous driving while under the influence, fourteen years in prison, which was the maximum amount for this type of crime. Maisy finally had justice for her babies, although she took no gratification in seeing their father jailed. His life sentence had started fourteen months ago when he had gotten into his car under the influence of alcohol.

Her parents hadn't been able to make the hearing, but she was very excited about seeing them at Christmas when they would be coming here to meet Jarrod and spend the festive time with them.

Maisy thought back over the last few months since she'd moved to Nags Head to try to make sense of her useless life. She'd been grieving so hard she thought it would never end. Something inside her hadn't wanted it to. For her, it had meant that if she were unhappy, she wouldn't forget what had happened. And she'd thought she had no right to happiness.

Then Jarrod had come back into her life. How could a girl be so lucky as to have had the memories of two beautiful children and then to be able to create a new life full of happiness? It was because one man, Jarrod, had made her see she did deserve to be happy. She did not have to be sad all the time; she thought of her children.

Her heart was full of love for him. She'd moved into his place permanently, and although they could live in Washington, DC, she liked it here, and so did Jarrod. He had finished renovating her house, and they had rented it out to a newlywed couple.

Elsa jumped off her when the jangle of keys hitting the table by the door told them Jarrod was home. Maisy wasn't far behind her and practically flew into his arms.

"I've missed you," she said as he picked her up and kissed her hard on the lips. The kiss softened, and her heart melted. She felt his breath on her neck as they parted, both panting.

She drew back slightly and put her hands on either side of his cheeks, his five o'clock shadow rough against her hands...she loved it when he hadn't shaved. She stared at him for a second and saw all his love for her in his eyes, and she couldn't help but steal another full-on kiss.

When they drew apart, he carried her to the sofa and sat down, cuddling her on his lap.

"Jarrod?"

"Uh-huh?" he said as Elsa nudged his hand and tried to jump on him. Then the pups started to wake up, and at the sound of his voice, they jumped all over them.

Elsa thought it was time for her to join in, and she plonked herself on Maisy's knee. Maisy giggled as that big, wet tongue of Elsa's licked her face and moved her head out of the way.

"Jarrod," she said, a little louder this time.

"Yeah, honey, what is it?" He played with the little ones, drawing his hand away quickly when they started nipping him. "Okay, you have my full attention," he said, looking her straight in the eyes.

"I'm pregnant." She held her breath for what seemed like minutes as she watched his face transform into the biggest grin she'd ever seen.

"Really?"

She nodded. "Really."

"Oh my God, Maisy." He gently moved Elsa off her lap and turned Maisy around so she could face him. He put his hand on her still-flat tummy and looked at it as if he were waiting for the baby to be born there.

She chuckled and lifted his head up with her fingers beneath his chin. In one look she saw her future: happiness and living with the man she loved. Elsa moved back to the pups, but not wanting to be pushed out, she licked Jarrod's face, and he laughed.

This was to be her life now. She'd been so lucky when she'd had her children, and when they were taken away she never thought she'd smile again. They were in her heart, so never would she forget the happiness they brought her.

She now had a second chance at happiness, and she was incredibly lucky to have found Jarrod again.

"Love you, always and forever," he said.

"Forever and always," she whispered back.

A word about the author...

Author Dilys J Carnie loves to write, usually contemporary romance, sometimes with a bit of suspense thrown in for good measure.

If she isn't in her office pounding the keys, she's settling into her favorite chair to read a book from one of her many best-loved authors.

Dilys is the proud mum of two grown-up children and two grandchildren.

She lives on the coast of Wales in the United Kingdom.

It is only two hundred steps to the beach from her home, where she lives with her cat Molly.

www.dilysjcarnie.com

Thank you for purchasing
this publication of The Wild Rose Press, Inc.

For questions or more information
contact us at
info@thewildrosepress.com.

The Wild Rose Press, Inc.
www.thewildrosepress.com

www.ingramcontent.com/pod-product-compliance
Lightning Source LLC
Chambersburg PA
CBHW060543260626
47161CB00003B/1032